BACK IN EDEN

BACK IN EDEN

•

Linda L. Paisley

AVALON BOOKS
NEW YORK

© Copyright 2001 by Linda L. Paisley
Library of Congress Catalog Card Number: 00-107009
ISBN 0-8034-9457-2
All rights reserved.
All the characters in this book are fictitious,
and any resemblance to actual persons,
living or dead, is purely coincidental.
Published by Thomas Bouregy & Co., Inc.
160 Madison Avenue, New York, NY 10016

PRINTED IN THE UNITED STATES OF AMERICA
ON ACID-FREE PAPER
BY HADDON CRAFTSMEN, BLOOMSBURG, PENNSYLVANIA

To our mothers . . .

Chapter One

The sun lowered in the west and colored the sky in a spectacular blend of pink and blue streaks. A long summer day neared its close. In the last half-hour before the darkness became complete, an evening breeze came up and wafted over two teenagers, a boy and a girl. In running shoes, shorts, and T-shirts, the pair jogged around a cinder oval track, a quarter mile in length, that sat in a natural bowl below Schoolhouse Hill, as the locals had named it long ago.

The girl felt the breeze drying her shirt where it was damp between her shoulderblades and at the small of her back.

They completed another lap of the circuit and her running partner said, "That's three. Another half mile, Willy?"

She nodded her assent, and they continued around the track. The shorter girl easily kept pace with her six-foot friend as he measured his stride to enable them to jog side by side.

After two additional laps around the oval, the runners continued to the baseball diamond's bleachers. Slowing their pace as they neared the seats, they did cool-down stretches before he collapsed onto a bleacher bench.

The girl tossed a white cotton towel to the boy.

"Catch!" she said with a smile, then leaned over to pick up her water bottle.

"Hey!" she yelled, as her friend snapped the towel across her backside. "That stung!" She straightened, turned, and splashed the contents of her water bottle at him.

"Well, that felt good!" Marshall laughed and offered her a drink of his water, which she accepted. She also accepted the bear hug that followed. Then they climbed the path that led up out of the bowl to the street, and walked toward her home. . . .

Willy jolted awake as the plane hit a patch of turbulence. Momentarily confused and slightly embarrassed, she half-heartedly returned the smiling glance of her seatmate, a forty-ish businessman. She had casually conversed with him during the flight which had originated in Houston, Texas.

Closing the mystery novel that she'd left open on her lap when she'd dozed off, she averted her eyes and gazed out the window at the cumulus clouds.

She was dumbfounded by the vividness of her dream. Had it been born of her apprehension at returning to her hometown for the summer? *That was foolish,* she told herself. She wanted to see her family, and Marshall didn't live there anymore. Even when he still had, they had managed to avoid each other well enough.

Back in Eden

Wilhelmina Grace Heidler's destination was Eden, a village in a largely agricultural area of Loramie County, Ohio. She had been born there to older parents and was the youngest by twelve years of three sisters. Her father, Joseph, passed away the year after she had graduated from college. Her mother, Grace, still lived in the family home, and Willy visited regularly during the four years she had been teaching at a high school in Katy, Texas.

As the plane began its descent, Willy took a compact from her purse to check her hair and make-up. She frowned at her reflection, then ran a comb through her tousled deep brown hair that she wore short, enhancing its natural ability to curl. Wide-spaced, chocolate brown eyes that slanted up at the outer corners looked worriedly back at her.

Her seatmate smiled and said, "Is there a young man meeting you at the airport, Ms. Heidler? If there is, he'll think you look lovely."

Willy smiled slightly and replied, "Thank you, but no, Mr. Kerr, I'm expecting my sister though."

The pilot made a smooth landing, and the passengers were soon filing out. Willy stood and straightened her cream-colored linen suit worn over a brown shell, then slung her brown leather purse over her left shoulder.

Stepping into the aisle, she thanked Mr. Kerr as he graciously handed down her carry-on bag. She then exited the plane onto the concourse and into the arms of her sister, Mary Caroline Granger.

"Hi, honey!" Mary said, giving her little sister a huge hug. Then, pulling back to look at her, "It's so good to see you again. You look marvelous!"

Willy smiled at her sister's typical exuberance.

"Thank you, Mary. You look great too! I like your new hairstyle," she added, touching the bouncy swing of Mary's short blond pageboy. Her blue print shirtwaist brought out the clear blue of her eyes.

"Thanks, love. I see that hot Texas sun has put light streaks in yours already. Your hair always did lighten up in the summer."

Continuing to talk as they walked toward the baggage collection area, Willy asked, "How are John and the kids? I can't wait to see everyone!"

"John is fine, only working too hard. Brent will probably look like he's grown a foot since Christmas, and Paige is at church camp this week, otherwise I'm sure she would have come with me to meet your plane. She's really looking forward to your being here most of the summer."

"I'm looking forward to being with all of you too. How is Mom doing since we last talked on the phone?"

"She's improving, Dr. Daw says. He won't allow her to leave the hospital though until her temperature stays down for a few days. Of course, the infection in her foot has upset the balance of her blood sugar, but that is coming along too."

"Good. I must admit that I've been worried about her. Though she's trying hard, I feel that she just hasn't been as well these three years since Dad died. But, I guess that's to be expected."

"Yes, his death was very hard on her. They were married for forty years, and I don't imagine they were ever apart for more than a few days during that whole time. But, it'll be good for her to have you with her. She misses you. We all miss you."

"I miss all of you, Mary, but I enjoy my life in Texas, too."

"I've never quite understood why you took a teaching position so far away, Willy. I would have bet that you would have stayed in Ohio, maybe even in Eden." Willy shifted a little uncomfortably as her sister added, "I actually thought that you would marry Marsh one day. You were so close once."

"Well, that was a long time ago. I did care about him very much, but you know that we were more like brother and sister as we were growing up."

Then, noticing the luggage coming onto the carrousel, she said, "Here we go. I've two pieces to collect and we can be on our way."

Engrossed in her conversation with Mary, Willy had not paid attention to the other passengers waiting near the turntable. Then, she reached for a large piece of brown leather luggage just as a strong well-manicured male hand enclosed her smaller one around the handle grip.

"Oh, I'm sorry!" she exclaimed, "I thought this was my bag."

The two of them lifted it off the carrousel to the floor, and the man checked the tag. "I'm the one who should apologize. Since my name is definitely not Wilhelmina Heidler, I believe yours must be." He smiled disarmingly at her.

"Yes, it is," she smiled back into the deep blue eyes of the nice-looking tall man whom she estimated to be about thirty years old.

They both turned back to the carrousel to watch for their luggage. Mary gave her younger sister a little poke on the arm from where she stood on the other side of her. Willy glanced her way and rolled her eyes heavenward at the mischievous grin on Mary's face.

The other piece of her luggage soon appeared. The pleasant man was still waiting when she and Mary left for the parking garage.

After getting on the Interstate, they soon left Vandalia behind and, heading north, passed by Tipp City and Troy before exiting the freeway to enter Piqua. Mary drove directly to Memorial Hospital, knowing that Willy was anxious to visit with their mother.

As visiting hours were still in effect, the sisters went directly to Grace's room. It was a typical hospital room, the walls pale green, the floor a highly polished gray-green tile, and a single window covered by green plaid drapes that were drawn against the brightness of the late afternoon sun. The sterility of the room was relieved by the row of get-well cards propped on the wide windowsill among two potted plants and a bouquet of pink roses.

They found Grace asleep in the bed nearest the window, the other bed unoccupied. Mary sat down in a nearby chair, and Willy stood beside Grace's bed, watching her mother's face while she slept.

Speaking quietly to Mary, Willy said, "She looks so frail lying there, even more so than at Christmas."

"I agree, but I'm sure she'll come through this just fine. She *is* getting older now; she was nearly forty when you came along, you know."

Willy sat down in a chair next to Mary's. "I wondered years ago if Mom and Dad were sorry they had me so late in life, and if they had regretted that I wasn't a boy."

"I know what the answer is, hon. I was fifteen when you were born, and I remember very well that they were overjoyed with their beautiful, healthy little baby daughter."

"Yes, Dad told me once that he didn't regret it for a minute and tickled my nose with the end of my braid. He said I kept him young and he called me 'his darlin' girl.' I think I'll never forget that evening. We were sitting in the porch swing out front." Close to tears, Willy searched in her purse for a tissue.

Mary reached over to hug her, didn't say anything, but kissed her on the cheek.

After wiping her face and blowing her nose, Willy added, "Maybe it's time I came back home to stay. Gretchen and Greg and their kids have to go where the Navy sends them, and you and John shouldn't have to shoulder all the responsibility for Mom, especially now that her health is more precarious. I'm single which makes it easier for me to move and to change jobs. Yes, that may be the answer for me and for Mom too."

"Well, little sis, don't make a rash decision. Talk to Mom first, and give it a lot more thought. Don't do it for John and me, just if it's what you want. I'd love to have you close by again, of course. You like Texas though. Would you be leaving anyone special behind?"

"Special? Yes, if you mean my students and friends, but if you mean a special man, no." Willy grimaced at Mary.

Mary smiled. "I thought not, or you would have told Mom or me by now."

"Yes, I would have. But, no such luck. I think your little sister is destined to become the proverbial old maid. Oh, I date some, but there hasn't been anyone to write home about, as they say." She ended with a big sigh. "Poor me!" she said, and giggled.

"Oh, your knight in shining armor will come riding up one of these days," Mary stated firmly. "I've no doubt about that."

From the direction of the hospital bed came a weak voice, but it was impossible to miss the affection in it.

"What are you two giggling about?"

Grace's girls got to their feet and went to stand on opposite sides of the bed.

"Sorry to wake you, Mom," Mary apologized.

"Hi, Mom!" Willy bent to kiss her mother's cheek. "We didn't mean to disturb you; you were sleeping so peacefully when we came in."

"I'm glad I woke up. I can sleep later after you have to go," the tiny gray-blond woman declared. "How was your flight, sweetheart? I'm very happy to see you."

Willy squeezed her slender hand and again worried that her mother was getting too frail.

"The flight was fine and right on time. Mary and I have only been here a few minutes."

"And giggling away, just like years ago." Grace responded with a smile, a twinkle in her blue eyes, her cheeks slightly flushed.

Mary replied, "We were discussing special men and knights in shining armor. And speak of the devil!" Mary added in an aside to Willy, as she looked past her shoulder to the door.

Willy whirled around and her mouth gaped as she recognized the man from the airport luggage area. Quickly closing her mouth, she said, "Oh, hello. What are you doing here?" Then, noticing his white coat, the stethoscope around his neck, and the patient's chart in his hand, she added, "You're a doctor?"

"Yes, ma'am!" He smiled, looking a little taken aback himself. "For the last five years or so, they tell me."

Feeling her cheeks pinken, Willy said, "I'm sorry, that sounded rude. I was just surprised to see you. Are you my mother's doctor?"

Her mother interrupted, "This is Young Doc Daw, as they refer to him around here. His father is Bill Daw, Old Doc, now that his son is on staff here. This is my youngest daughter, Wilhelmina Heidler, and my older daughter, Mary Granger."

"I'm pleased to officially make your acquaintances," he said as he smiled and shook the hand of both ladies in turn. "I'd noticed that the name on the chart was Heidler as on your luggage tag, but had no idea I'd see you here." His broad smile indicated that he was pleased at the coincidence.

"To answer your question, Ms. Heidler, I'm assisting my father with some of his cases, so I'm doing his evening rounds."

"It's nice to meet you again, too, Dr. Daw," Willy replied in a subdued voice.

The doctor turned to Mrs. Heidler. "How are you feeling this evening? Any complaints that I should note for Old Doc to see in the morning?"

Grace smiled at him. "No, I'm feeling much better, and the nurses are treating me royally."

"Their notes on your chart indicate that your temperature is nearly back to normal, and your blood sugar levels are stabilizing also."

He turned to the nurse who had followed him into

the room. "If you ladies will step into the hall, I'd like to check the ulcer on Mrs. Heidler's foot for myself."

Mary gladly escaped into the hall, not being up to looking at the condition of the sore.

Willy asked if she could stay. "I'll be looking after my mother when she's released, and I'd like to see the ulcer now to be able to judge better the progress of its healing later."

He looked at her in surprise. "Are you sure?"

"Yes, and I'm not inexperienced completely. Mother had a diabetic ulcer several years ago while I was still living at home in Eden."

"Yes, I was aware of the previous ulcer," he replied. He bent over the foot in question and quickly unwrapped the bandages. "Look closely and you can see evidence that it is starting to shrink in size."

Placing a small basin under the foot, he cleansed the affected area with a sterile solution. Then, he deftly applied wet-to-dry sterile pads and rewrapped the foot.

Willy closely watched the process, then smiled at her mother. "It's coming along, Mom. We're doing just fine."

"Yes, dear, and thank you, Young Doc," she said to the young man who was thoroughly washing his hands at the sink in the corner of the room.

"You're welcome, Mrs. Heidler." He nodded at the nurse who was gathering the used supplies, and she left the room.

After making a note on Grace's chart, he bade her goodnight. Taking Willy's elbow, he politely asked her to join him in the hall.

Mary returned to her mother's room, but not before tossing a questioning look at her sister as they passed in the hall. Willy responded with an "I don't know" expression.

They walked a few paces farther down the hall before he released her elbow and turned to face her.

She looked up at him apprehensively. "It *is* coming along well, isn't it, Dr. Daw?"

"Oh, yes, I didn't mean to imply otherwise. Please, would you call me Bill? I also share my father's first name, thus another reason for the "Old Doc"–"Young Doc" routine. May I call you Wilhelmina?"

"Certainly. I was worried there for a moment; you seemed so serious as we left the room."

"I was serious; I was seriously considering whether to ask you out to dinner, and if there would be even a slight chance that you would accept."

He smiled coaxingly as he looked down at her pretty face, which relaxed into a smile of its own at his question.

"Yes, I'd like that, Bill. When were you thinking of going?"

"I'd say tonight, but I still have rounds to complete. And, I know you just got in today, so how about Saturday night?"

He doesn't waste any time, she thought. Aloud she replied, "That would be fine. Would it help if I drove into Piqua to save you the trip out to Eden and back?"

"Thanks for the offer, but I'll pick you up at your mother's home. I assume that's where you're staying since you mentioned you'll be caring for her later."

"Yes, it's at 210 East Sycamore just to the right of Main Street. Eden is so small, I don't think you could get lost." She smiled as he took her hand in his.

"I'll be there by seven o'clock, Wilhelmina, barring emergencies. Goodnight."

"Goodnight," she replied. She watched his tall straight form in the white medical jacket as he walked toward the nurse's station. *An interesting man*, she observed, as she returned to her mother's room.

"What did Young Doc want, dear?" Grace asked.

Noting the concern on her mother's face, Willy quickly replied, "It's fine, Mom. It didn't concern your health at all. In fact, he wants me to call him Bill and to have dinner with him Saturday night."

"Aha! I knew it!" exclaimed Mary with a gleeful chortle, as she turned from the roses she had just arranged in fresh water. "I thought I detected signs of interest in you, first at the airport, and then when he came into the room here. Have you found that knight already?"

Willy blushed, but she answered casually. "Oh, I don't know about that, but at the very least I'll go out to dinner with him, and probably have a very nice time."

She and Mary pulled straight chairs up beside Grace's bed and explained how they'd met the doctor at the airport earlier.

Later, they sensed that Grace was becoming tired, so they told her goodnight, assuring her they would both stop in Friday afternoon. Her mother asked for her purse from the bedside table and found her car keys, handing them to Willy.

"I know you have a house key, but please use my car to get around while you are here, dear. Your father would say it's not good for it to just sit in the garage."

"Thanks, Mom. You have a good sleep tonight. See you tomorrow." She kissed her forehead, then Mary did the same.

Outside in the hospital parking lot, Mary suggested

that they grab a sandwich before heading for Eden. "John is playing golf with some business friends this evening, and Brent is picking up a few dollars caddying, so I won't see either of them until after eight-thirty, maybe nine."

Willy readily agreed. They were soon seated in a booth at a fast-food restaurant where they enjoyed diet-breaking chocolate shakes and cheeseburgers.

"I feel so sinful," Mary said, smiling across the table. "Since I've passed forty, I tend to gain weight so easily that I really have to watch it."

"But aren't all these calories delicious?" Willy said, grinning in return.

On the drive up the winding state highway to Eden, Willy rolled down her window and enjoyed the fresh country air blowing through her hair. As they drove past the fields and farmhouses that she had known since girlhood, she asked numerous questions about whether this family or that still lived here or there.

"Old Jim Petersen died since you were home at Christmas, but perhaps Mother told you that. No one lives in the house now, but the family still owns it," Mary replied. "The old Brown place is sitting idle now also."

Willy looked sharply at her sister's profile outlined against the glow of the western sky where a colorful sunset was forming.

"I—I didn't know that."

"Don't you remember? Lela Brown died about a year ago, and Ed Brown went to live with his daughter in Columbus. The farm has been on the market for six months or so. I don't think it has sold."

Willy sat in silence as her mind wandered back

through the years to the woods on the old Brown place. She and Marshall walked along carrying fishing poles. He wore cut-off jeans and sneakers, and his shirt was tied around his waist. In his other hand was a bait bucket.

She was in shorts, sneakers, and a halter worn under a button-down shirt. She could even remember that the shirt was white and the shorts and halter were green. They stopped in a clearing where she sat down on a fallen log to take off one damp sneaker. . . .

"Did you hear me, Willy? I was saying that I put fresh linens on your old bed yesterday so you'll be able to get right in when you are ready for bed."

Mary's words pulled Willy from her reverie. "Oh, thank you, Mary. That was thoughtful. I *am* a little tired."

"When mother went into the hospital, I removed the perishables from her fridge. I should have replaced them yesterday as well, but I didn't get to it."

"That's fine. I don't need much, and I'll enjoy a walk to the grocery tomorrow."

By this time, Mary was turning from Main Street onto Sycamore and soon pulled into the driveway of the Heidler house, a two-story white frame with green shutters and a wide front porch. The two women toted the luggage from the back of the station wagon into the house and up the stairs to Willy's old room.

"No matter how long I'm away from Eden, this room always feels like home to me." She walked around the room which was wallpapered in a blue flowered print. She ran her hand over the maple dresser, picked up and hugged a well-worn teddy bear from the window seat, then touched the starched white Priscilla curtains at the west window.

"The sunset is lovely tonight," she mused, then turned to her sister. "Thanks, Mary, for meeting me at the airport and all."

"My pleasure, hon. I'm glad you're here safe and sound. It'll be good for Mom to have you with her this summer. I'm very thankful that you were able to arrange to come home. But, I'd better be on my way back to Piqua. Before I know it, my men will be home."

Willy trailed Mary down the stairway and, after a quick hug on the porch, she watched and waved as her sister backed out of the drive and drove away.

In the gathering twilight, she could see Mrs. Harper, her mother's longtime next door neighbor, on her porch swing.

"Hello!" she called.

"Hello, Willy! Welcome home. How is Grace doing?"

"Dr. Daw had only good things to say. She'll be home soon."

"I'm happy to hear that. You tell her I miss her, and that her cats are doing just fine. I've been putting out a little milk and dry cat food each morning for them," the lady added by way of explanation.

"Thank you, Mrs. Harper, that's very kind of you. I'll tell her tomorrow that you asked about her. Goodnight."

Mrs. Harper waved goodnight, and Willy went inside, closing and locking the door behind her.

She spent a few minutes wandering about the house. She peeked into the living room to the left of the front entryway, and then crossed back to the door on the right. Opening that door, she stepped into her father's den. Everything seemed almost the same, and Willy could still sense his personality in that room. She sighed and closed the door, then walked down the hall to her mother's cheery kitchen. Nothing had changed very much since she had left home for Texas.

She noted that though Mary had forgotten to stock the refrigerator, she certainly had given the house a thorough once-over. All was tidy, freshly dusted and swept. *Bless her sweet heart.*

Remembering the cats, she went to the back door, opened it and called, "Cleo, Cleopatra! Desiree! Come on in, girls!"

In moments she had two very affectionate felines purring and rubbing their soft furry bodies against her legs. "Hello, darlings! How are you, Cleo? And you, Desiree? Are you glad to see me? I'm very glad to see you."

Willy stooped to pet and cuddle the cats. Cleo, the older, was a sleek black short-hair with green eyes; Desiree was an eight-year-old seal point Siamese with gorgeous blue eyes and a haughty manner. Then, inviting them inside, she found a can of soft cat food in the cupboard and served up a portion for each of them.

Later, after the cats had licked their dishes clean, she told them goodnight and put them back outside for the night. Locking the backdoor, she turned off the lower floor's lights and tiredly climbed the stairs.

After unpacking only what she would need for the night, Willy opted for a relaxing bubble bath over a quick shower. Removing her traveling clothes, she thought, *it looks as tired as I feel*, as she hung the rumpled linen suit on a hanger on the back of her door.

Slipping into the shiny bubbles in the white tub, she

slid down until they reached her chin, rested her head back against the end of the tub, and closed her eyes. *Now don't fall asleep and drown*, she warned herself, smiling as the warmth of the water began to soothe the tiredness from her limbs.

As she relaxed even more, her mind drifted back to Brown's Woods and Marsh. She saw him as if it had been yesterday. His dark brown, nearly black hair a little shaggy, his hazel eyes flecked with green smiling up at her as he knelt to check her little toe that hurt as she walked. "It's just a tiny cut from a sharp rock, when you were wading, probably," he teased her, his voice soft and gentle. "You'll live, Willy."

He leaned down and kissed her toe. She knew he was just kissing it to make it better, but she felt such a shock that she gripped the log to keep her balance. His body stiffened. He looked again at her face, and his eyes held a look that she had never seen before, outside of a movie screen.

What's happening? He's never looked at me like that before!

She heard the slight clink as the two fishing poles slid from where she'd propped them beside her on the log. Marsh leaned up onto his knees before her, pulled her into his tanned arms, and kissed her in a most unbrotherly manner. . . .

Willy forced her mind back to the present. She mentally chastised herself. That had been the most humiliating day of her entire life. She was glad that Marsh lived in Cincinnati now. She could be here with her mother, enjoy seeing old friends and neighbors, and not have to worry about running into him.

She rose from the cooling tub, toweled herself dry, and slipped into light cotton pajamas.

Outside, a tall, slender, dark-haired man in blue jeans and a black T-shirt paused on the sidewalk before the Heidler house. Hunkering down, he petted the cat that crossed the yard to him.

"Hello, Cleo. How are you, old girl?" he asked in a quiet voice. "She's home, isn't she? The light's on in her old room. She just fed you, too. I can smell the fish on your breath." He chuckled softly at the friendly, purring cat.

Rising, he jammed his hands into his back pockets and stood a few minutes longer, lost in thought.

"Goodnight, Willy," he whispered into the darkness, before he walked slowly down the street.

Chapter Two

A tired Willy fell asleep easily in her comfortable old double bed, snuggled under the blue chenille spread and snowy white sheets.

Awaking not long before dawn, she turned to her travel clock beside her bed. Hearing the long whistle of a train as it approached on the tracks near the center of the village, she realized how much she'd missed that sound, especially in warm weather with her bedroom windows open, as they were tonight. As a girl, her mind often trailed off on imaginary rail journeys to fascinating destinations.

Turning onto her right side, she said good morning to the teddy bear still sitting on the window seat. Jumping out of bed, she strode the few yards to pick him up, then brought him back to bed with her. Hugging him close, she said, "Have you missed me, Sweetie Bear? Thanks for holding down the fort while I've been living in Texas. It's not your fault I didn't take you with me. You just remind me too much of Marsh and that day at the county fair when he won you for me."

The stoic teddy bear looked back at her, and Willy grinned. "Nothing to say on the subject, huh?"

She gave the bear a hug and scooted down in the bed, planning to go back to sleep.

Instead, sleep didn't come, and her mind soon wandered to thoughts of Marshall Gray.

She and Marsh, his younger brothers, Marc and Marty, and a group of other kids were playing a pickup game of softball on the diamond in the field behind the schoolhouse one summer day when she was thirteen.

It was her turn at bat, and she took a mighty swing and miraculously connected. The ball flew over Marty's head in center field. Softball not being her best sport, Willy stood astounded at home plate, her mouth gaping as she watched the ball sail away.

Marsh yelled, "Run, Willy!" Then, when she still didn't move, he picked her up in a fireman's hold and ran around the bases with her while the other kids hooted and hollered.

"Put me down, Marsh! Right now!" she yelled as she pounded on his back and kicked her legs, getting angrier by the second. Back at home plate, Marsh set her on her feet. Red-faced and fuming, she took a swing at him. Of course, he ducked but fell flat in the dust around home plate, laughing at her. Even angrier at his laughter, Willy stalked off, but Marsh came after her.

"Aw, come on, Willy! Don't be mad. I was only kidding around." He laid an arm around her shoulders, which she huffily shrugged off, then walked on.

They heard the other kids calling them back to the game.

"Hear that? Don't spoil it for the other kids, Willy."

At that, she stopped walking and turned back to face Marsh, her hands on her hips, her pony tail swinging.

"Okay, but don't you dare do that again, you—you silly goose!"

Marsh tilted his head to one side, grinned, his hazel-green eyes sparkling, and teasingly said, "My, my, what strong language. Silly goose, huh?"

She grinned sheepishly in return, then Marsh grabbed her hand, and together they ran back to the game. . . .

She was thinking of Marsh too much lately. She supposed it was because she was back home. Willy turned over in the bed, punched up her pillow, and tried to doze a little longer.

An hour or so later, she stirred and stretched her legs out the length of her bed, wriggling her toes in the process. A ray of early morning sunshine fell across her face. She said to herself, "Up and at 'em, girl. Lots to do today."

She made her bed and returned Sweetie Bear to his place of honor on the window seat. Flying down the stairs, she called Cleopatra and Desiree from the back-door.

Taking their can of cat food from the refrigerator, she served them their breakfast, then looked around for something for herself. She filled the teakettle to heat for instant coffee, then dropped two pieces of whole wheat bread into the toaster.

Finding a pad and pen on the kitchen counter, Willy

checked the maple cupboards and the refrigerator then jotted a list of things she could use in the next few days.

When the toast popped up, she spread some margarine and orange marmalade on it, then poured the now hot water over the coffee. Stirring it thoroughly, she sat down at the table covered with a bright sunflower-patterned tablecloth to eat.

I should have called Betsy last night, Willy thought. Checking the wall clock, she noted that Betsy would still be at the apartment they shared in Katy. She went to the phone in the hall. Dialing the number, she sat down on a padded bench next to the phone, ready for a chat with her friend.

"Hi, Betsy! It's Willy." After a pause, "Yes, the plane was on time, and my sister met me at the airport."

In reply to Betsy's question, "She's getting better, but I don't yet know when she'll be released from the hospital."

Then, "Thanks, roomie! I'll tell her later today. Oh, here, let me give you this number." Having done so, Willy told her friend goodbye, knowing Betsy had to get to work, then hung up the phone.

Rising, she returned to the kitchen, rinsed her cup and plate, then let the cats back out.

"Have a good day, girls. See you later."

Taking the stairs two at a time, Willy finished unpacking her bags. After a quick shower and shampoo, she wrapped a large towel around herself and studied her reflection in the mirror. She didn't look as stressed as just before the trip home. Seeing her mother made her feel better. Reassuring herself that Grace would come through this latest illness just fine, she toweled her hair partially dry.

Willy realized that being home in Eden was part of the reason she felt so much more relaxed. She loved this little town. When her mother was better, she planned to talk with her about staying. One of the high schools in the area might still have an opening for next term. She still had her Ohio teaching certificate, or she could work at something else for a year. She decided it was worth speaking to her mother about the possibilities.

Back in her bedroom, she slipped on panties and a sports bra, denim shorts, and yellow cotton T-shirt. Putting on white cotton socks and her most comfortable sneakers, she then applied some moisturizer to her face, hands, and legs. Adding some lip balm, she spritzed on her favorite lilac cologne, and with a hairbrush tidied her hair. She decided to let it air dry on the way to the grocery.

Transferring her wallet and keys to a fanny pack, Willy picked up her list from the kitchen and left by way of the front door to walk to Gilardi's Grocery.

The morning was beautiful, and her spirits rose even higher as she walked briskly along the sidewalk, admiring the neatly mowed lawns and blooming flowers and shrubs in the neighborhood. The tall leafy trees, a mix of maple, oak, elm, cottonwood, and an occasional pine, shaded the houses and the sidewalks.

A wave here and there or a hello from people who were already out in their yards or whom she passed on the street, added to her feeling of coming home.

Gilardi's Grocery had changed over the years. It now had the look of a supermarket, though still smaller than its city counterparts. Willy went inside and wheeled a cart through the aisles, selecting the things on her list and a few additional items that she found on special for the week.

At the checkout stand, she greeted Agnes Simms, a middle-aged lady who had worked at the grocery for as long as Willy could remember.

"How are you, Agnes?"

"Well, hello, Willy! How nice to see you again. Folks around here wondered if you'd be coming home this summer. How's your mother doing?" She was still a friendly and caring lady.

"Much better. I'll be seeing her again this afternoon," Willy replied as she placed her purchases on the counter.

"Good. You tell her I send my best wishes. Your mama's a special person, you know," Agnes added with a smile.

"I think so too, and I'll be sure to tell her you asked about her."

After paying for her groceries, Willy picked up the paper bag, then paused at a bulletin board next to the exit. She glanced over the ads of used items for sale, yardwork and babysitting services offered, as well as apartments and rooms for rent. Then her eyes fell on a poster to one side announcing a dance to be held at the Eden Community Hall on the following Friday evening. The Eden Volunteer Fire Department and Emergency Squad were sponsoring the dance as a fundraiser.

"Agnes, I see there's to be a dance next Friday. I haven't danced for ages. It might be fun to go."

"Yes, you should go, darlin'. You never know who you might see there. A pretty girl like you will have plenty of likely dance partners."

"Well, maybe. But, yes, I think I *will* go! Why not?" She smiled back at Agnes and gave a determined nod, bouncing her now dry curls.

Saying goodbye, she left the grocery and walked home, her step light, just like her heart.

After putting her purchases away, Willy grabbed a pair of her mother's gardening gloves from a shelf on the backporch. Walking across the backyard, she inspected the neatly spaced rows of vegetables, decided to weed the green beans, and bent, literally, to the task.

An hour or so later, after having gone on to the carrots and beets, thinning the rows to allow for the growth of the sturdier plants, Willy took a break, stretching her back. Walking over to the shade of two large maple trees at the back of the yard, she flopped into a wide hammock that was suspended between two sturdy branches.

Pushing off with one foot hanging over the side, she swung back and forth. It felt good to work in a garden again, she thought, as the steady sway of the hammock relaxed her until she nearly fell asleep. But, no, Desiree decided to join her in the hammock, followed closely by Cleo, and any thought of a nap fled as the girls insisted upon being petted and fussed over.

"Hello, you little devils. What have you been up to this fine morning?" she asked as she stroked their soft fur. "No answer, huh?"

The three of them rested a while longer, before Willy felt thirsty enough to go inside. After drinking a glass of cold water, she checked the time and realized why she felt hungry.

Opening a can of chicken noodle soup, she got down the cracker tin, and opened the bag of ready-to-eat baby carrots she had purchased that morning.

When the soup had warmed in the microwave, she placed the bowl on a tray along with the crackers and carrots, grabbed a spoon and napkin, and carried the tray into the living room. Turning on the television, she watched the noon news from the comfort of her father's brown leather lounger while she ate.

Halfway through the program, her hand, holding a carrot, stopped midway to her mouth. Her eyes stared at the screen as she concentrated on what she saw there.

"Oh no, what is Marsh doing on TV in Piqua? He's supposed to be working in Cincinnati," she murmured aloud to the room.

He was being interviewed about a legal case, she gathered, and it was definitely coming from Piqua. She told herself not to panic, but the admonishment didn't stop the tremor that ran through her or steady her breathing.

Willy knew that there was an outside chance she'd see him. After all, his parents still lived in Eden, and she had accidentally run into him over the years a few times.

Despite her anxiety at seeing him, Willy drank in the sight of him. He was still as good-looking as ever, she thought, admiring his trim dark hair and the stubborn jut of his well-defined jaw. The flash of his hazel-green eyes as he talked spiritedly about some cause appeared even greener when he felt strongly about something or someone. He looked thinner though, and he seemed somehow different. Despite herself, she wondered what had been happening with him.

Enough of this, she reprimanded herself as she got up and turned off the set. There were things to do, and one of them was definitely not sitting and mooning over Marsh. She had adored him once, and they had been the best of friends, but things changed. Their lives changed. They were virtually strangers to one another now.

Carrying her tray to the kitchen, she washed the dishes and put away the uneaten crackers and carrots.

She climbed the stairs to change for the drive into Piqua, but her step was not quite as light as it had been.

Back downstairs, clad in tan cotton slacks and a green jungle print camp shirt tucked in at the waist, and wearing brown leather sandals, Willy found the gardening shears and went outside to her mother's flowerbeds. Cutting a few stalks of late iris, she returned the shears and wrapped the stems in a damp paper towel. Choosing a vase from the pantry, she went to the garage and backed out her mother's Chevy Corsica.

Checking the gas gauge, she stopped at Grilliot's Garage on the south side of town.

"Hi, Augie! Please, fill it up."

"Right away, Miss. Oh, hi Willy! Gosh, I should have realized that was you driving your mother's car."

"Yep, it's me. I got in last night. Going to spend some time with Mom while she recuperates. In fact, I'm headed to the hospital now."

Talking while he worked, the station attendant hooked up the gas hose to her tank, then cleaned the windshield.

"Be sure to say hi from me when you see her. I hope she's back home real soon."

"I will, Augie."

"That'll be twelve-fifty," the young man, a son of

the station owner, said as he took off his billed cap, wiped beads of perspiration from his forehead onto his denim shirtsleeve, then replaced the cap.

Willy handed him a twenty-dollar bill, and he quickly returned with the change.

"So long, Willy, and thanks."

"Bye and thank *you*."

Thirty minutes later, she had parked in the visitor's lot at the hospital, taken the elevator up to Grace's floor, and was greeting her mother.

"Good afternoon, Mom. How are you today?" she asked as she bent to kiss Grace's cheek, pleased to find her awake and sitting up in bed.

"Hello, dear. I'm doing fine, don't worry. Are these for me?"

"Of course, silly," Willy smiled, "who else am I visiting?"

Grace admired the three perfect purple iris blooms that Willy had brought.

"These are from my flowerbed, aren't they? It must be about the last of the blooms."

"Yes, they are. I'll put some water in this vase I brought along."

Doing so from the sink in the corner, Willy set the bouquet on her mother's bedside table then took a chair next to her.

"What did Old Doc say this morning?" asked Willy as she set her shoulder bag on the floor by her chair.

"Well, I'm still running a bit of fever, but that should get better in a day or so. I told him that Young Doc had asked you out, and he seemed quite pleased with the idea. His comment was something like 'smart boy.' " Grace smiled and patted Willy's arm.

Willy grinned. "Well, I haven't seen Dr. Daw, Old

Doc, for several years, but I guess it's nice to get his approval, so to speak!"

"Did you get all settled in last night?" asked Grace.

"Yes, mostly, but I saved some unpacking for this morning. I got re-acquainted with Cleopatra and Desiree. They hadn't forgotten me at all."

"Of course not!"

"This morning, I called Betsy, and she sends her best wishes, as does Mrs. Harper. I talked to her for a few minutes last evening. She'd been looking after the cats. Then I walked to the grocery this morning, and Agnes hopes you'll be home soon. As does Augie, whom I saw when I stopped to gas up the car."

"How nice of all of them," Grace replied as she pressed her hand to her lips, coughing lightly.

Willy held the water glass so the straw reached her mother's lips. "Are you all right?"

After taking a few swallows, her mother replied, "I'm fine. Just a tickle in my throat. What else have you been doing?"

"Well, after grocery shopping, I weeded in the garden and thinned the beets and carrots. The cats joined me for a nice swing in the hammock before lunch, which I ate in front of the TV set as I wanted to watch the noon news." Willy paused for a moment, compressing her lips, as if considering whether to go on.

"What? I didn't see the news. Was there something upsetting?"

"No, not to anyone else, anyway, just to me," she admitted and smiled wanly at her mother.

"Marsh was being interviewed on TV about a case he was working on, and he was here in Piqua. I thought he had stayed in Cincinnati after law school?"

"He did, as far as I know. I haven't talked to his

mother for a good while, since January, I believe. She did say at that time that Marsh was having some problems, but she didn't elaborate."

Willy, looking agitated, rose, walked to the window and stared down at the back service area of the hospital complex.

"Well, looking at him, I felt something wasn't quite right. It made me wonder if something had happened to him."

"Perhaps you should get in touch with him while you're here. You were such good friends once, nearly inseparable while you were growing up. You've never really talked with me about it, but I sensed something had gone wrong around the time he went off to Ohio State. I never wanted to pry, but if ever you want to talk about it, I'm here for you. I've always hoped you've known that."

"Oh, Mother, yes, I know that," her daughter said emphatically.

Turning from the window, Willy moved to the bed and squeezed Grace's hand.

"You're right, Mom, things did go wrong. My feelings were badly hurt. We never did really talk about it, just skirted around it. Then, in a few days, he was off to college. After that, when we saw each other, we were polite, but that's it." She fought back the tears she felt stinging her eyes.

Her mother pushed the tissue box closer to Willy, saying, "Go ahead, have a cry. Sometimes it's the only thing that helps."

That's just what Willy did, then wiping her tears, she apologized. "I'm sorry, Mom. You don't need this right now. You've enough to handle as it is."

"Nonsense, dear, I just wish you had spoken of it

long ago. Please, do consider what I suggested. If you are both in Eden or the area, now may be the right time to talk."

"Perhaps, but it won't change anything, you know." Almost choking on the words, Willy added, "He's a married man now."

As a nurse came in to check Grace's pulse and temperature, Willy excused herself, saying she needed to visit the ladies' room. Her mother nodded, knowing her daughter wanted to clear away the evidence of tears.

When Willy returned to the room, Mary had arrived to visit also, and the three of them had a nice time talking. Telling their mother goodbye when it became evident that she was ready for a nap, the sisters left the hospital.

Walking to their cars, Mary invited Willy to come home with her for dinner. "You haven't seen Brent and John yet, and at seven I'm driving down to Camp Maple Grove to pick up Paige. She'd be delighted if you came along too."

"Great! Thanks for asking, Mary. I can help you with dinner."

"Not doing anything fancy. Some chops on the grill."

They soon arrived at the Granger home, a brick two-story dating from the Civil War era, on North Downing Street. The sisters reminisced while they prepared a cool salad and potatoes which Mary pre-baked in her microwave, then wrapped in foil to finish roasting on the grill.

Willy related some funny happenings at her school in Katy, and Mary talked glowingly about how much she enjoyed running her own interior decorating business during the past year, long a dream of hers.

John and Brent joined them shortly after five. They found them on the patio relaxing with tall glasses of iced tea.

Willy hopped to her feet to give her fifteen-year-old nephew a big hug.

"Your mother said you'd grown taller since I saw you last, and she was right," exclaimed Willy, giving the blond, blue-eyed youngster a kiss on the cheek which the boy returned with a loud smack.

"Almost up to six feet, Aunt Willy, and I can tower over you now!" He laughed as he patted his five-foot-six aunt on the top of her head.

"But not quite over *me,* at least not yet," inserted Brent's father, as he loosened his necktie. "Hello, Willy, it's good to have you here again."

Willy returned her brother-in-law's gentle hug and smiled. "Thank you, John, it's good to be back home. I was thinking just this morning how happy it made me to be in Eden again."

Within a half-hour the chops and potatoes were ready, and they sat down to dinner around a patio table that John and Brent had slid into the shaded area.

While they ate, the four caught up on one another's most recent activities. Willy learned that Brent had been working in some advanced tennis lessons around the part-time job he held as a box boy at a supermarket.

"I'm planning to enter the summer rec league's annual city tournament later in the summer in the "under sixteen" category," Brent said, sounding more than a little excited about the event.

"Super, Brent! Hope I'll still be here so I can see you play," his aunt responded.

"It'll be held in August, Willy," said her brother-in-law. "Brent and I have been playing singles a couple evenings a week, partly to give him the extra practice and partly to keep myself in shape," he added with a chuckle as he served himself a piece of the strawberry pie that Mary had just brought out from the kitchen.

"Mmm! That looks really good, Mom," Brent said.

"Oh, by the way, I ran into Marshall Gray last week. Didn't you and—what?" John exclaimed, looking sharply at his wife—reacting to the quick little jab to his shin that she had given him under the table.

Willy felt a tightening of her stomach, but she managed a smile. "That's okay, Mary, John. I haven't seen Marsh for several years, not since he married."

"Well, I'm sorry, John. I shouldn't have kicked you," Mary apologized. "But yesterday at the airport, when I mentioned Marsh, Willy seemed to not want to talk about him, so I—"

"It really is okay," Willy repeated. "I know Marsh is here in Piqua, as I saw him on the noon news today, just by chance. I suppose it's just a temporary assignment to work on some case. He's been with a firm in Cincinnati for the last three years or so."

"If you haven't seen him, how do you know?" asked her nephew, with the directness of youth.

"Brent!" his mother said warningly as she shot him a "watch your mouth" look.

"Sorry, Aunt Willy."

She reached across the table and squeezed his hand where it lay on the tabletop. "While I haven't had any personal contact with him, Brent, his mother writes to me occasionally, and she told me where he's living and working."

"I got the impression, from our conversation, that he had left the Cincinnati firm and was planning to work here now. He's going in with old Bertram Jones who wants to slow down and turn some of his work over to a younger man," said John.

"Really?" Mary said in surprise. "Bertram Jones seems to specialize in championing the underdog. Is that the type of work Marsh would want to handle, Willy?"

Willy, whose thoughts had wandered to Marsh while her sister and brother-in-law talked, felt her heartbeat increase at the sound of his name. Pressing her hand against her stomach as if that would ease the tension she still felt, she took a deep breath.

"What?" she asked, looking at her sister. "Oh, yes, Bertram Jones. Marsh has known Mr. Jones since we were teenagers. They used to have long talks, and Marsh looked upon him as a mentor."

She paused, idly pushing around a few bites of pie left on her plate, then spoke again. "I believe it was through Mr. Jones's influence that Marsh decided to study law. I'm not surprised that Marsh would want to work with him."

Mary glanced at Willy, who was still watching her fork move around her plate, then asked John, "I'm curious, did he mention his wife?"

"No, I don't recall that he did. What's her name?"

"Alicia," Willy stated, forcing a smile to her lips and rising from her chair. "May I help you clear things away, Mary, before we go to pick up Paige?"

Mary and John exchanged a quick glance, and Mary, realizing Willy wanted to change the subject, said, "Yes, please. It will soon be time to leave. Are you coming along, John, or you, Brent?"

Brent begged off, saying his friends Chad and Jeff were coming by later to play pool.

"All right, son. I'd like to come along, ladies," John replied with a smile. "It's been awfully quiet around here this week, hasn't it?"

The others laughed at his reference to the absence of his vivacious thirteen-year-old daughter.

Chapter Three

With Willy in the backseat and Mary beside him, John drove the station wagon through the fairly heavy Friday evening Piqua traffic. Picking up a westbound highway, he followed it for a few miles, then made a left turn onto a state route and headed south.

Willy enjoyed seeing the area again as she had not been through there in several years. A short time later, John turned off the highway onto a county road and soon pulled into a crowded parking lot near an old and weathered red-brick country church.

"Oh, it's hardly changed at all!" Willy exclaimed as they exited the car and looked around.

Indeed, the stately old church did look much the same as when Willy had come to church camp there about fifteen years earlier. While no longer serving as a church, it was still owned and maintained by a denomination in the district and drew campers from a large area. The building now was the headquarters of Camp Maple Grove, obviously named for the beautiful stand of sugar maples on the grounds. It contained meeting rooms, a kitchen, a dining room, and, of course, the original sanctuary in which daily chapel service was held when camp was in session.

Directly before Willy was the large open field that was used for softball and soccer. A black-topped rectangle stood to one side set up with basketball hoops and stanchions to hold a volleyball net.

On the far side of the field, several hundred feet behind the church, was a smaller building, a stone one-story where craft classes were held. Farther away, across the length of the recreation field, stood the white frame cabins with a shower house set between them. Though she couldn't see them because of the trees, Willy knew that behind the first cabins stretched a line of three more, the ones nearer the river for the girls and the row higher up the hill for the boys.

The placid Stillwater River flowed by in a southerly direction. A swimming pool, definitely not Olympic-size, had been built on the opposite side of the river and could be reached by walking across a bridge.

All this Willy observed in just a few seconds as she and Paige's parents walked forward onto the grassy area where several dozen other campers' families had gathered.

A group of jeans-clad girls emerged from the path that led alongside the lower cabins, and Willy waved her arm high in the air as Paige screamed, "Aunt Willy!" The slender girl broke from the group and ran across the field as her parents and aunt walked out to meet her.

Giving first her mother, then her father a quick hug, Paige threw herself at her aunt, whose arms encircled her affectionately.

"Gosh, Aunt Willy, it's good to see you! When did you get here? How long are you staying?" The girl bubbled with enthusiasm at seeing her aunt. Paige had missed her very much since she moved to Texas.

"Hi, sweetheart. Just yesterday, and I don't know how long I'll be staying yet. You look just great, Paige," she added, as she released her brown-eyed, dark-haired niece and held her at arm's length to look at her. "The sun has streaked your hair like it always seems to mine."

"Yes, it has," Paige replied as she gave her pony tail a little twist with her right hand, grinning at the others.

"Have you had a good week, hon?" asked her dad.

"It's been super, Dad. Lots of fun, and I've met lots of new kids. I've got addresses so I can write to Susie, Candi, Grant, and Jill."

Her father picked up on that one name and raised his left eyebrow while squinting his right eye at his daughter. "Grant?"

"Yeah, he's from Greenville, Dad, Mom. He's a really neat boy. You'd like him too, I just know."

The girl grinned at the three adults, blushing a little as they all looked back at her.

"I'm sure we would, Paige," responded her mother.

Willy said through a definite giggle, "Boy, does this bring back memories. I remember meeting a boy from Tipp City here at camp and writing to him for a year or so. It was fun."

John smiled, and Mary said, "I think I did that, too. He was from just west of Dayton, and his name was Andy. Yes, Andy Henderson."

"Hm-mm," murmured her husband.

"Oh, shush, John, you and I didn't even know each

other then!" Mary turned to him with a teasing grin. "He was an awfully cute boy as I recall."

John gave her a hug. "Seems all of you Heidler women caught boyfriends at this camp. Must be something in the well water."

At that, they all laughed. Paige was more than a little pleased to be included in the phrase *Heidler women.*

Willy volunteered to walk back to Paige's cabin to help her carry her things to the Granger car. They had returned and had stowed everything in the back when the senior boys' counselor, Kent, called for everyone's attention.

"Welcome to our last evening here at Camp Maple Grove, at least for this fine group of campers. The week has been very enjoyable, for the leaders as well as the campers, we hope."

This statement was met with cheers and a rowdy round of applause from the boys and girls who had gathered on the recreation field.

"As our final activity," the young man continued, "we will hike to the site of our evening campfire and vespers. By the time we reach it, the sun will be nearly down. The campers have been instructed to keep their flashlights with them for this one last time."

Paige held hers aloft, as she'd kept it with her when she'd stowed her things in the car. Mary, knowing the camp traditions at Maple Grove, pulled a small flashlight from her purse.

"Now, if your parents or your ride home hasn't arrived yet, Dirk is going to stay behind to direct them to the campfire area. So, let's form up by cabins starting with number one nearest the crafts building and spreading across the field toward the blacktop. Okay?"

The troop followed a dirt and gravel path that cut to the river side of the girls' cabins. It closely followed the river for about an eighth of a mile, then began to climb. The hikers abandoned their two-by-two formation as the path narrowed, demanding single file walking. At some time, past campers had gathered medium-to-large rocks and lined the outer edge of the path with them for safety.

It soon grew darker under the thickly leafed trees that lined the path. They reached a steep drop and many flashlights were switched on. Here a wooden handrail ran along a crude stairway built of flat rocks set into the hillside. At the bottom of the steps, two of the counselors tended the evening campfire in a large open area. Arranged around the firepit were logs and large rocks, and the adults were directed to find a place to sit, while the campers, for this evening, sat on the packed-down grass.

"Everything seems the same, doesn't it, Mary?" whispered Willy to her sister.

"Yes, it's nice to know not everything changes."

After Kent, the counselor, brought forward Liz, the head girls' counselor, the two of them introduced the remainder of the staff to the parents and other adults gathered at the campfire.

Annie, the official song leader, and Liz soon had the campers singing with the adults joining in on songs they also knew. Willy was surprised at how much she remembered of the old camp songs and hymns she had learned in her youth, and how much she enjoyed singing them again.

Her mind wandered to similar campfires held so many years ago. She sat on a log with Carolyn and Jenny, two of her cabinmates, and Marsh sat across the campfire from her. While the fire was high, she couldn't see him, but as the fire died down, she looked his way and found him gazing across the fire at her. The sound of the group singing seemed to fade away from her consciousness, and all she saw was Marsh. She felt happy as they both smiled, and he winked at her. . . .

Willy came back to the present with a sigh and joined the singing of "Down in My Heart" and "Do Lord" which Annie led in three-part rounds. As the fire died down, the leaders thanked the campers for a good week and the parents for joining them for the evening. After a prayer of thanksgiving and hope for the future, a final song of parting was sung and the gathering, still singing softly, trekked back to the main camp area.

That same evening in Eden, Marsh took a break from laying new linoleum in his kitchen. Taking a can of cold beer from an ice chest, he went out to the wide front porch on the old farmhouse, sat down on the top step, tipped his head back, and took a swallow.

Placing the can on the step beside him, Marsh raised his arms over his head, flexed his tired back muscles, and stretched his long legs out and down the few steps. Looking above the woods that stood on either side of the gravel lane that ran from the farmyard to the road, he sat quietly admiring the rose-colored western sky as the sun sank.

Pulling up his knees, he rested his head upon his folded arms for awhile. His thoughts drifted over the past few months and his marriage.

"What a mess I've made of things," he muttered.

"Though when we married, it seemed the right thing to do." But, he was glad he had divorced his wife. Staying in Cincinnati even a month longer would have been self-destructive. He knew he couldn't have handled living with Alicia any longer, having learned what he now knew.

The type of cases assigned to him at the high-powered law firm her father ran with an iron hand were definitely not to his liking. Marsh was disgusted with pampering rich clients, and handling child custody and divorce cases. He hadn't worked his backside off in law school to practice that type of law.

He snorted derisively. But here he was with a divorce of his own, not something he'd thought would happen to him. He ran his hands through his dark-brown hair as he recalled the last time he and his wife had talked.

Marsh came home to find Alicia dressing to go out.

"Hello, Alicia," he said as he slipped out of his suit jacket and removed his tie. "Going out?"

"Yes," she replied, catching his eye in the mirror where she was applying mascara to her light blond lashes. "I don't know what you're doing tonight, but I have plans to meet Jayne later."

"To do what?" he inquired testily, though a part of him could guess.

"Why do you care?" she snapped back at him. Smoothing her ash blond hair back from one side of her pretty face, she inserted a gold clasp behind her ear, allowing the rest to fall freely to her shoulders.

Marsh bit back the reply he had nearly made. Instead, he let her vent her ill-humor.

She slipped into a pair of three-inch black heels.

Back in Eden

"Anyway, it's no longer any business of yours what I do, so don't pretend you care," Alicia said spitefully.

"I really *don't* care anymore, Alicia, but I wanted to talk to you this evening." Marsh kicked off his shoes, unfastened his cuffs, and pulled his shirttail from his waistband.

"So, talk." Alicia smoothed her mid-thigh black skirt over her shapely hips, then turned back to the mirror. "I'm leaving in fifteen minutes."

"All right. I'll make this fast," Marsh said, his voice even and controlled. "I handed in my resignation this afternoon. I'm accepting Bertram Jones's offer, and I've made a bid to buy that farm near Eden that I told you about."

Alicia's back stiffened, but her expression remained cool. "I see. Well, I hope you're very happy there, alone," she said pointedly. "I've already told you what I think of that little hick town."

"Yes, I'm well aware of that. In fact, if you'll go into your father's office tomorrow, you can sign the divorce papers. They're drawn up and waiting, as we'd discussed. I've already signed them. Your father has read them, so I'm sure they'll be acceptable to you. Ed Cathcart will represent you in the divorce, and as your father will most likely supervise him, you should have no problem."

"Sounds like you've taken care of everything, but it may not be as easy as you seem to think," she said as she picked up a fur wrap and small clutch purse. Stalking to the door, she turned, her hand on the knob, "Pack your things, Marsh. I don't want you here when I get back."

"I've already started," he retorted as she slammed the door behind her. . . .

Marsh sighed, reached for the can of beer and drained it. Rising to his feet, he took one last look at the sky.

"Red sky in the morning; sailor take warning. Red sky at night; sailor's delight." Marsh recited the old adage that his deceased grandmother had often quoted. "I'm not a sailor, but it looks like a fine day tomorrow, Grandma." With one last flex of his back muscles, he returned to his kitchen.

Saturday morning, Willy awoke slowly from a dream. She and Marsh were dancing at a school dance; the quick steps they did left them a little breathless, but laughing as the song ended.

They applauded the student combo that provided the music, and as the next tune, a slow number, began, Jerry Ellison, a boy Marsh's age, approached and asked her for a dance. Marsh stepped back, and she danced with Jerry, but she was aware of Marsh leaning against a wall to the side of the gymnasium the whole time. She stole a peek over Jerry's shoulder a few times, and her brown eyes collided once with Marsh's greenish ones. She couldn't read his expression, but he gave her a rather wistful smile, and her heart leapt.

He's . . . no, he can't be, but I'd almost swear that he's jealous, Willy thought. Amazed at her discovery, she missed Jerry's next comment. She answered with a noncommittal little "hmmm," hoping she wasn't getting herself into anything. . . .

As Willy threw back the sheet and sat up, swinging her legs to the side of her bed, she groaned. What had made her have that particular dream?

"No use trying to figure that one out," she mumbled drowsily as she stepped into her flip-flops and headed to the bathroom.

Sometime later, after showering and dressing in denim shorts, a coral T-shirt, and her trusty sneakers, Willy fed the cats, and then had a bite of breakfast. Before putting things away, she decided to pack a lunch to take with her on her planned hike around town.

With the lunch stowed in her fanny pack, Willy strode west down Sycamore to cross Main Street, which was also a busy state highway. She waited as a tractor-trailer truck approached and passed her with a honk of the horn and a wave and big grin from the driver.

Well, I guess some things just don't change, she thought with a smile, recalling the many times that had happened to her as a teenager.

After crossing Main, she walked a few more blocks and turned onto Tulip Lane, where her aunt and uncle, Hilda and Karl Heidler, lived. No one answered the doorbell, so Willy took a chance on finding someone in the backyard.

"Hello," she called as she rounded the corner of the two-story yellow frame house. "Anyone home?"

"Willy!" her aunt replied from near a flowerbed as she straightened and turned toward her niece. Pulling off her gardening gloves and shoving them into a pocket of her green smock, she said, "How nice to see you, dear. Grace told me you were expected the other day when I visited her. How are you?"

Willy accepted and returned her aunt's warm hug. "I'm just fine, Aunt Hilda. Happy to be back in Eden again."

"I assume you've seen your mother already."

"Yes, I got in on Thursday and have seen Mother twice. I had dinner at Mary's last night and rode along to pick up Paige at camp last evening. So, I've been busy, but I wanted to stop to see you and Uncle Karl today. I hope you've been well?"

"We can't complain, dear. Just the usual aches and pains that come with getting older. My, but you look pretty. I guess Texas agrees with you."

Willy laughed. "I do like it there. I've been realizing though, since I've been back, how much I've missed Eden. I feel so at home here; I can really relax. Perhaps that's because I was worried about Mother before I got here, but I do find it less stressful, being back home."

"Well, dear, perhaps that word *home* is the key." Her aunt smiled kindly at Willy as she added, "If your heart is here, possibly you should be too."

Willy blinked. *Could she be right?*

Aloud, she said, "Is there anything I can help you with while I'm here?"

"No, thank you, at least not at the moment. The morning's getting warmer, so I'll put my gardening tools away for now." The stout-figured lady in her late fifties removed a straw hat and fanned her face with it. "Would you like to have some lemonade?"

Willy spent the next hour on Hilda's cool and pleasant front porch relaxing in a comfortable chaise lounge. While they shared lemonade and homemade oatmeal cookies, they caught up on family news and the local Eden gossip.

"Do you remember Ginny Evers, Willy? Well, she's Ginny Morgan now and just had twin babies in April. One of each. Cutest little things."

"Yes, I remember her. Goodness, twins," Willy replied, as she recalled that Ginny was several years younger than she. *Oh well. Maybe someday.*

She was brought back from her musing by Aunt Hilda's next words.

"Frank Gray came into the hardware store the other day, Karl said. It seems Marshall has taken a job with old Bertram Jones in Piqua. Frank said that he and Eva were pleased to have him move back to the area."

Willy swallowed a sip of lemonade to hide her reaction to the mention of Marsh's name.

"Yes, I'd heard from John that Marsh was in Piqua. John had run into him recently."

"I always liked that boy. Seemed so bright and thoughtful. His parents think the world of him, and rightly so," Hilda said.

"Yes, I remember him well. He was a good friend to me when I was young." She managed to sound cool and calm.

Changing the subject away from Marshall, Willy said, "Thanks for the scrumptious cookies and lemonade, Aunt Hilda. I'll get back to my walk now. I want to go by the church and cemetery."

Hilda held the screen door open as Willy carried the tray into the house and set it on the kitchen counter.

Taking a pair of shears from a drawer, Hilda said, "Follow me to the backyard, dear, and we'll cut some flowers to take to your father's grave. I have some late-blooming iris that are just perfect."

"How nice. Thank you so much, Aunt Hilda," Willy said a few minutes later, as she wrapped the stems in a damp paper towel that Hilda offered. "Say hello to Uncle Karl for me, and I'll see you again soon."

Willy left with a wave of her free hand, and walked

north up Tulip until it curved back to Main Street. Turning left, she followed it to Church Road. Taking the county road, she passed a few fields, the community hall, and the volunteer fire department building. About a quarter of a mile along, she topped the rise on which stood the red brick church that she remembered so well.

This place brings back so many memories, she thought as she looked around and up at the tall spire that held the church bell. She opened the metal gate set into an opening in the thick, but well-clipped hedge that surrounded the cemetery.

Wending her way among the headstones, Willy paused at her father's gravesite.

"Hello, Papa," she whispered. "I'm home again."

Stooping, she upended the metal vase that was set into the base of the marble stone between her parents' names. Willy retraced her steps, crossed the county road, and entered the older section of the cemetery. Near a maintenance shed she pumped some water into a bucket at an old well, then filled the metal vase.

Back at the Heidler marker, she set the vase into its holder and arranged the lovely purple and white iris.

"These are from Aunt Hilda's garden, Papa. They're so pretty." Willy sat down on the grassy area near Joseph Heidler's grave. "I miss you. I've been thinking of staying in Eden rather than returning to Texas, but I know I must give it more thought. Work out all the pros and cons, as you would say, but I may stay."

Leaning her head on her propped knees, she ran her hands through her short, wavy hair. "Marsh seems to be moving back to the area. I know, Papa, if I stay here, I'll have to work out how I feel about him. Of course, he's married now, so there's no future for me with him, but I do have to face up to that fact."

Raising her head, she reached forward and traced her father's name and dates on the pinkish-gray marble stone. In her mind she remembered her father saying, "It does no good to run away from life, Willy."

"Is that what I've been doing, Papa? I thought teaching in Texas was my way of having an adventure, but have I really just been running away from something? I was hurt once. Have I been afraid of being hurt again?"

Rising from the ground, she brushed off the seat of her denim shorts. "Mom has urged me to talk with Marsh while we are both in the area. Perhaps I should."

With a last look at her father's resting place, she turned away and left the cemetery. Within a few minutes, she was nearing the intersection of Church Road and Main Street. Without hesitation Willy crossed Main, turned north, and after a few blocks made a right onto Brown Road.

She soon left the village behind and walked at a brisk pace on the gravel at the edge of the pavement. Shortly after crossing the bridge over a small creek, she climbed a hill at the top of which Brown Road met Eden Road.

Without even thinking about it Willy followed Eden Road a little way until it crossed over the Loramie River. At the bridge, she took a well-worn path down an embankment and followed the trail along the riverbank downstream to the east.

She hadn't been down the path for years, but it looked nearly the same as it had the last time. As she completed that observation, she rounded a thick patch of raspberry bushes. There before her was Marsh's favorite fishing hole.

A feeling of *déjà vu* washed over Willy. Two young people, a boy and a girl, both teenagers, were fishing. The boy, dark-haired, leaned his back against the old cottonwood tree, his long legs stretched out before him. The girl, blond hair in a pony tail, sat crosslegged on the riverbank, reading a book while she kept one eye on her pole.

Willy watched them for a moment and felt a tug at her heartstrings. *My goodness, it's like seeing Marsh and me ten years ago.*

She took a deep breath, then called out, "Hello, any luck today?"

The girl turned her head quickly, the pony tail bouncing. "Oh, hi," she replied with a friendly smile.

Willy walked forward and joined them on the riverbank.

The boy checked his pole, then stood up and stretched his lanky body. "Just a few nibbles today," he said.

"I'm Willy Heidler. I used to fish at this same spot years ago. Marsh, my friend, was the serious fisherman, but he liked for me to come along for the company. I would more likely be reading or wandering around." She smiled warmly at the young people.

"This is a good fishing hole usually," the boy, about fifteen, replied. "Marsh? Is that Marsh Gray? I've met him. In fact, he stopped and talked to me one day a few weeks back when he found me fishing right here."

The girl, a little younger than the boy, had stood up and joined them. "I'm Dusti Dunaway and this is my brother, Jack. Are you related to the Heidlers who have the hardware store?"

"Yes, my father and Uncle Karl ran it for many years together. I'm visiting my mother, Grace Heidler, for the summer. I'm happy to meet both of you."

"Pleased to meet you too," Dusti replied.

"Well, I'll be on my way. Bye. Hope you catch something."

"Thanks, so long," the youngsters answered as they returned to their previous spots on the riverbank.

Willy began to retrace her steps, but instead took another less worn path that led toward a woods. She moved into the pleasant shade where the path veered between two large oak trees.

She probably shouldn't go through the woods, she thought. She knew she was trespassing, but it *was* getting hot, and the shade felt so cool and pleasant. She laughed at her obvious rationalization. She just wanted to walk in Brown's Woods again.

Willy continued to follow the trail through the trees, enjoying the sound of a slight breeze rustling the treetops and the occasional birdcall. Her eye caught the flash of a red cardinal, seemingly leading her down the path as it flitted from tree to tree just ahead of her.

Presently, she crossed a little brook on stepping stones and continued walking. She breathed deeply of the aromatic scent of pine boughs as she ducked under a low-hanging branch of a tall tree.

She stopped where the trees thinned out, forming a sun-filled open area. Willy paused and looked about before walking forward to sit on a fallen log.

Unbelievable. The spot hadn't changed. It was still peaceful and quiet. She sat for several minutes and absorbed the solitude.

She closed her eyes and thought of that day when Marsh had kissed her. It seemed so long ago now, but she'd never forgotten a second of that day, even though sometimes she'd tried.

She and Marsh were fishing at his favorite fishing hole. He sat on the bank leaning his back against the cottonwood tree. She was several yards further upstream looking for colored rocks. She removed her sneakers to wade into the shallow water along the edge of the river because her eye had caught the sparkle of something shiny. Bending over with her back toward Marsh, she reached her hand into the water.

"Ouch!" exclaimed Willy at the sharp sting of something hitting her rear end. "What was that?"

She turned quickly and looked toward Marsh. He hadn't moved from his spot under the cottonwood tree. Just the fact that he hadn't looked at her made Willy suspicious.

"Marshall Gray!" she screamed as she jumped back onto the bank.

"Hey!" he yelled as she ran at him. He rolled away from the tree in one fluid motion.

"You threw a rock at me! That hurt, you big bully."

"You made such a perfect target, I couldn't resist aiming at it," Marsh laughed. "Besides, it was just a little pebble, and you were splashing around and scaring the fish."

"Oh, pooh! You've been saying that to me for ten years."

"And you've never listened in ten years, have you?" He tugged on her ankle and she abruptly sat down beside him.

"No," she admitted through a spasm of giggles as he grabbed a foot and tickled her bare sole. She kicked out with her other foot, but Marsh ducked and only laughed at her attempt to connect with his arm.

Willy giggled again. "Marsh, stop it! You know I hate to be tickled."

"I know. That's why it's so much fun," but he quickly released her foot. With an odd look on his face, he moved back to his spot under the tree near his fishing pole.

Willy was left to wonder about his sudden change of mood. Frowning, she got up and returned to the book she had left laying on the riverbank....

The quiet was broken by the chatter of a squirrel peeking down at her from a hickory nut tree.

"Hello, you noisy little fellow. Are you hungry? Or are you stuffed full of last year's leftover hickory nuts?"

Remembering her own lunch stowed in her fanny pack, Willy unfastened it from her waist and got out her sandwich and small water bottle. She bit into her favorite sandwich, peanut butter and sweet pickles. Willy tore off a small piece and tossed it to the ground so that it landed a few feet in front of where she sat on the log.

Sitting quietly, she waited, and soon the curious squirrel became emboldened enough to dash down the trunk of the tree and across the open space to the bread. Tucking it into a rounded cheek, he flashed back up the tree, reappearing on the overhanging branch.

Willy laughed aloud, a lovely clear sound that carried through the woods on the slight breeze.

"Well, you didn't waste your chance, did you, little fellow? Faster than a speeding bullet; it's Super Squirrel!" she said to the bright-eyed critter as she watched it retrieve the hunk of bread and begin to chew on it.

* * *

Marsh had walked to his parents' home and was strolling back up his lane when he stopped dead in his tracks and listened. The hairs on the back of his neck prickled at the sound of clear, female laughter being carried on the breeze. Marsh looked toward the trees on his left and, after only a moment's hesitation, entered the woods, moving quietly through the trees.

He paused in the shadow of a large buckeye and looked into the clearing. *Willy.* He stood for several minutes while his eyes feasted on the girl he had not seen for years.

She looked wonderful to him, even lovelier than he had remembered her. He watched the movement of her slender throat as she tipped her water bottle to drink. He admonished himself for spying on her and took a step forward, intending to make his presence known.

However, he hesitated when he saw her fumble in a pocket for a tissue and wipe her eyes. Marsh looked away. He felt uncomfortable as he knew she wasn't aware of his presence. He wondered what was wrong, but he knew he had no right to intrude on her privacy.

He gave her one last, sad look, turned and quietly slipped away.

Willy had eaten the sandwich and sipped a little of her water when she suddenly felt so melancholy that she dissolved into tears. *What's the matter with me?* She searched through her shorts pockets for a tissue. She could usually control her feelings, but lately she had become such a weeper. She decided that she shouldn't have stopped here. There were too many memories in this lovely spot in the woods.

She stiffened suddenly and looked around the clearing. She heard a twig snap, but she didn't see anyone. She thought that she'd better be moving on if she were going into town to visit her mother that afternoon, and refastened her fanny pack.

Willy walked down the path toward Eden Road and, after having made a large loop through the village, arrived back at her mother's house.

Chapter Four

Shortly before six that Saturday evening, Willy was in her bedroom looking over the summer dresses that she had brought with her from Texas.

"Maybe," she murmured, as she pulled out a black and white geometric print made in a sleeveless style with a V-neckline. Since, she wasn't sure where Bill and she were going for dinner, she felt the jersey knit with her black linen blazer over it would do nicely.

Having made that decision, Willy took the jacket downstairs to her mother's laundry room where she ironed out the few wrinkles that remained from being packed in a suitcase.

After a quick shower she dressed in the outfit. Tempted to go without pantyhose, she decided to conform, but wrinkled her nose at the pair as she began to work them on.

A few minutes later, she brushed her short, fluffy hair and applied a little blush and rose lipstick. Adding a gold chain with intermittent black and white beads, she spritzed on a little lilac cologne and declared herself ready.

Glancing at her wristwatch, she lightly glided down the stairs just as the doorbell rang. Seeing Bill Daw, looking cool and handsome in a tan summer suit, standing on the other side of the screen door, made Willy glad that she had taken extra care with her appearance.

"Hello, Bill," she said with a welcoming smile as she unlocked the screen door and opened it wide for him. "Come in."

"Good evening, Wilhelmina," Bill returned her greeting as he stepped into the hallway. "How pretty you look."

Willy grinned impishly as she gave a mock curtsy. "Thank you, sir. Not knowing what restaurant we would be at, I didn't want to underdress too much."

"I should apologize for not calling you about that," Bill stated, "but, as usual, I got busy at the hospital."

"That's quite all right, no harm done," Willy replied good-naturedly. "Would you like to sit down, Bill, or do we have a reservation?"

"Yes, for seven-thirty at the Bellingham, so we probably should go."

Willy picked up her white purse that matched her two-inch sandals and said, "I'm ready then."

When they had settled into Bill's car, a sporty black two-seater, Willy asked, "Where is the Bellingham, Bill? That name is new to me, but then I've been away for several years."

"So have I," he smiled as he picked up speed, having left the village, and headed north on the highway. "The restaurant's near Harris Mills. When I asked Dad to recommend a nice place, he suggested it. Said if he were taking you out to dinner, that's where he would take you or any other pretty girl." Bill glanced over at her.

"My goodness, I'm surprised that your father remembers me. The last time I was in his office was probably in high school when he set a broken finger." She smiled at the memory.

"I'm curious, how did you break a finger?"

"Oh, I was on the girls' soccer team. I was playing goalie and broke this one in a mad scramble for the ball." She lifted and wiggled the index finger on her left hand.

"Looks fine now," he commented. "So you were into sports as a girl?" Bill asked as he turned right onto the route that would take them into Harris Mills, the county seat of Loramie County.

"Yes. Soccer in the fall, basketball in the winter, and I ran track in the spring. I suppose I was something of a tomboy, but in a small high school such as Eden's was at that time, almost every available body was needed to field a team. I did enjoy the physical activity of sports though."

"And the competition?" Bill asked with a lift of his eyebrow.

"Oh, yes, that too. Did you take part in sports in high school and college, Bill?"

"Some. I was on the swim team and golfed in high school, but found I hadn't enough time for either in college. I did continue to compete in swimming for my freshman year, but my pre-med course at State dictated that I drop it later."

"I can understand that," Willy commented with a little grimace. "Never having been very good in science courses in high school, I avoided them as much as possible in college. Thus, my major in social sciences."

"Where did you attend college, Wilhelmina?" he inquired as he slowed for the turn into the grounds of the Bellingham Inn.

"Miami at Oxford. I got my teaching credentials four years ago and have been working in Katy, Texas, since then. I teach American history and government classes at the high school level," she replied.

Having pulled into a parking slot, Bill came around to her side of the car and opened the door. She took his offered hand as he helped her out, and he continued to hold it casually as they walked to the covered entryway that led to the door of the restaurant.

The building was a one-story affair of rustic design and constructed of stained wood and fieldstone. Set in a grove of trees, it blended nicely with its sylvan surroundings.

They were soon ushered to a table for two covered with a pink tablecloth and laid with sparkling silver and crystalware. It sat next to a wall of glass that allowed an uninterrupted view of the beautiful wooded area that spread out from the back of the building.

"What a lovely place," Willy exclaimed.

"Dad said that he spotted a deer gliding through the trees a few weeks ago when he and Mother were last here."

"Oh, I hope we see one tonight," Willy said eagerly as she peered through the glass.

Bill smiled across the table at her as she turned back to him and returned his warm smile.

"What?" she asked, when he didn't say anything, but continued to look at her.

"Oh, just that you're such charming company, Wilhelmina. So refreshing and open."

"Goodness, you embarrass me," she looked down shyly before looking up at her companion again. "I'm enjoying your company too, Bill, and please, call me Willy. Most of my family and friends do, though Mother sometimes falls back on my given name."

"All right, Willy, but I rather like your full name. It's unusual. Is it a family name?"

"Yes, my father's mother was Wilhelmina Irene. I'm Wilhelmina Grace, the middle name for my own mother, of course," she explained.

"As you already know, I'm a junior. William Edmond, Junior, to be exact. At times it's confusing, especially now that I've gone into practice with Dad. Perhaps my parents should have called me Ed rather than Bill. It would have made life simpler, but I'll just have to put up with being Young Doc, I guess."

Signaling the waitress, he asked Willy if she would like a pre-dinner drink.

"No, thank you, Bill. I am hungry, though, I must admit," she added as she looked over the menu. It had been a long time since her peanut butter and pickle sandwich in the woods. She quickly dismissed the thought, as it made her think of Marsh, and she did not want to do that tonight. Returning her attention to Bill, she heard him say to the waitress that they would order now.

"I'd like the chicken Kiev," Willy said, "with rice and asparagus alongside."

She heard Bill order the lamb kabobs with wild rice. Willy studied his cleanly chiseled profile as he spoke to the waitress. Easy to talk with and handsome too.

A tiny sigh escaped involuntarily from Willy's lips as he turned to her and spoke.

"Now, what were we talking about? Names? But tell me about Katy, Texas, Willy."

She did just that. She told him of the school and some special students. When their food was served, he urged her to continue, so she talked about the Future Teachers of America chapter that she advised and the girls' soccer team that she helped coach.

"Purely as an assistant to the regular coach," she emphasized. "I work more in the area of stats and scouting, but I enjoy being involved with the girls and the sport."

"You certainly keep busy," he remarked before taking a sip from his water glass. "Do you miss Ohio at all, Willy?"

"Yes, at times, I do very much. When my father died after I had been in Katy for a year, I very nearly gave up my job to move back to Eden to be with my mother. But she wouldn't hear of it. Didn't want me to disrupt my life for her, she said, but I would have if she would have allowed it."

"Your mother is a lovely lady. I've enjoyed getting acquainted with her in the past year that I've been back in Piqua."

"Thank you, I agree. But you've been back longer than I'd realized," Willy remarked as she dabbed at a corner of her mouth with a burgundy napkin.

"Yes, I joined Dad about this time last year after completing a residency in Internal Medicine at Johns Hopkins."

"Oh, when we met at the airport, I don't know why, but I assumed that you had just come back to Piqua."

Bill smiled across the table. "No, I'd been in Houston for a conference that took place earlier in the week. We'd been on the same plane the whole trip. I noticed you."

Willy felt her cheeks flush. "Oh! I'm afraid I was a little pre-occupied on the flight. I was anxious about my mother."

"Understandable. I hope seeing her has helped to allay your anxieties?" Bill asked as he worked the last chunk of lamb from his skewer.

"Yes, it has. You know, it feels so good to be back in Eden. I've realized how much I've missed that small town quality of life. Less hustle and bustle, I suppose, and it is so nice to better know your neighbors."

"I agree, Willy. I'm enjoying being back in Piqua also. A much less harried pace than Baltimore."

He suddenly looked past her and out the window, as a movement had caught his eye. "Look, Willy, the deer has come back."

Willy quickly followed his gaze and gasped in delight. "Oh, she's beautiful!" And then, when a fawn no more than a few months old joined its mother beneath the trees, Willy clasped her hands together at her chest. "Look, Bill, her baby is with her. So sweet."

Bill, who was watching Willy watch the deer, thought he definitely agreed that she was sweet. And lovely, and fun, and intelligent.

They lingered over a second cup of coffee before leaving to drive back to Eden.

"It's been a lovely evening, Bill," Willy said as they turned onto Sycamore Street. "Thank your father for recommending the Bellingham."

"I'm glad that we got to see the deer," she added when he had stopped the car in the Heidler drive.

"So am I, Willy. I really enjoyed this evening. I hope we can spend more time together while you're here."

"That would be nice," Willy replied, then, as Bill came around to her side of the car and opened her door, she impulsively added, "Do you like to dance, Bill?"

Taking her hand to help her from the car, he said, "Well, I haven't danced for years, but I used to enjoy it a little. What do you have in mind?" he asked a little warily.

She smiled up at him encouragingly as she stepped from the low-slung car. "Well, there's a dance next Friday here at the Eden Community Hall. It's a fundraiser for the volunteer fire department. It'll be very casual and a mix of square and round dancing. I plan to attend, and if you're interested, perhaps we could go together?"

"Yes, let's do that. Of course, you know you're risking bruised toes as my dance steps are pretty rusty."

She laughed aloud as they walked up the sidewalk.

"I'll take the chance, Bill." Then, "Good evening, Mrs. Harper," Willy called when she noticed the porch swing next door moving in the semi-darkness.

"Evening, Willy," her neighbor answered.

Bill smiled as they reached the porch. "Thank you for having dinner with me, Wilhelmina Grace Heidler. It was a very pleasant evening."

"For me, too, Bill. I'd invite you in for a bit, but I'm sure Mrs. Harper, knowing that I'm alone in the house, wouldn't approve." She returned his smile.

As she unlocked the front door, he chuckled, "Remember what we were saying earlier about small town neighborliness?"

"Uh-huh, Mrs. Harper probably still thinks of me as a little girl in braids." Willy laughed, but spoke quietly. "Not old enough to date, let alone invite a man inside."

"Do you suppose she'd mind if I kissed you goodnight?" Bill whispered, his lips close to Willy's ear.

"Well, actually, I don't believe she can see us," she whispered in return.

Taking that as a yes, Bill lightly brushed his lips against her left cheek. She turned her face up a little to him. This time he kissed her lips, gently but thoroughly, with a certain degree of restraint.

Willy lightly returned his kiss.

"Sweet," he murmured, then added, "Goodnight, Willy. When should I come by next Friday?"

"Oh, the dance," she responded a little distractedly. "It starts at eight, but we can go at anytime."

"Then, I'll see you around eight. I'll call if I can't get away from the hospital for some reason."

"All right. Goodnight, Bill."

She stepped inside and hooked the screen door behind her, then watched him walk to his car and back out of the drive.

A nice man, good company, fun and handsome, and a doctor to boot. Most any girl would be ecstatic to date him. *Then, what's the matter with me*? She had enjoyed his kiss, but there was no electricity. No more so than with any of the other fellows that she'd dated in college or since.

Heaving a huge sigh, she closed and locked the door, then climbed the stairs to her bedroom. She slipped out of her blazer and dress and hung them up before going down the hall to the bathroom where she brushed her teeth and cleansed the make-up from her face.

Returning to her room, she picked up Sweetie Bear then stretched out across the bed with him cuddled in her arms.

"Hello, old friend. I had a pleasant evening out with a very fine man, but I feel depressed. I probably shouldn't have suggested the dance. If we aren't going to develop into anything, I should discourage Bill's attentions rather than encourage them."

Willy rolled over onto her stomach with another sigh. She remembered that one kiss she had shared with Marshall so many years ago. Perhaps she should stop comparing all other men's kisses to that one. But no one else's had ever made her feel like that one kiss had.

Marsh had married someone else, and she needed to get past him and the way she felt. She wanted a husband and children. A home of her own. She wondered if she could fall in love with Bill. Could she, if she gave him a chance?

With her thoughts still in a muddle, she stood and removed her underwear, slipped into her pajamas, and turned off her bedside lamp.

Marshall, restless as evening approached, often walked into Eden from his farmhouse. He invariably passed the Heidler home, and tonight was no exception. Noticing that the house was dark, he turned into a tiny park across the street and sat on the top of a picnic table, resting his feet on the seat while he struggled with his thoughts.

He knew that he wanted to talk with Willy. He

wanted to know how she'd been, if she was happy in Texas. Why was she crying when he had seen her in the woods? Was she worried about her mother? Or was it something else?

He wondered if there was a way to become friends again. He felt he should find a way to make amends for his past actions. Now, while she was here for the summer.

He raised his head at the sound of a car approaching and watched it turn into the Heidler driveway. The driver cut the engine and lights. Despite the gathering darkness, Marshall could tell that it was not Mrs. Heidler's Chevy. When he saw a tall man get out and then open the other door, Marshall knew it would be Willy emerging from the passenger seat.

She'd been out on a date, and something seemed to twist inside him. *Don't be a fool, man, of course she dates,* he told himself. She hadn't been living in a nunnery the past ten years.

He heard the clear sound of her laugh as they walked up to her porch, and then her greeting to Mrs. Harper.

Marshall told himself that he should leave. Not good form to be watching them, and probably Mrs. Harper had seen him as he went by her house. Maybe it'd be better that he just stay out of sight now that she's back.

Marshall stayed where he was, sitting atop the picnic table until after the car had gone and Willy had turned off her bedroom light. By the time he left the little park and continued his walk back to his home, he had made a decision as to what he must do if he were to gain any peace of mind where Willy was concerned.

*   *   *

Sunday morning came. Willy awoke shortly after dawn to the twitter of songbirds in the linden tree that grew tall outside her bedroom window.

She lay quietly for awhile, enjoying their sound. Her mind replayed the previous evening's dinner date with Bill Daw.

She had enjoyed his company. He was interesting, and he had seemed interested in her. At least for the summer, she mused, as he knew she planned to return to Texas. Would it be wrong for her to spend time with him? Should she give them a chance to get to know one another better? Perhaps feelings for him could grow, if they just let their lives progress naturally. Wouldn't that be the best way?

Willy threw back the sheet and stretched as she stood up. Somehow, she felt as if she was on the brink of discovering something important. As she walked down the hall to the bathroom, she remembered that her father had always said, "Trust in the Lord, Willy, and He'll never lead you astray." Willy smiled a little wistfully. "Oh, Papa, I wish you were here now."

After looking over the Sunday newspaper while she ate a light breakfast and fussed over Cleopatra and Desiree, Willy tidied the kitchen before going back upstairs to prepare for church.

Having dressed in a simple fitted cocoa sheath that skimmed her slender figure, Willy tied a lightly woven fringed scarf in a delicate cream around her shoulders. Slipping into her brown leather sandals, she picked up her shoulderbag and checked that she had moved her wallet and keys from her other bag before going to the garage.

Willy greeted several old friends and neighbors as

she made her way from the car toward the door of the country church on the hill. The bells began to ring overhead as she stepped inside.

Accepting a bulletin from the teenager who was handing them out in the vestibule, she paused to say hello.

"Good morning. It's Dusti Dunaway, isn't it?"

The girl responded with a wide grin.

"Hi, Miss Heidler. Nice to see you again."

As there were people behind her, Willy merely smiled and continued into the sanctuary. Pausing to look around, she saw Aunt Hilda and Uncle Karl about halfway down the left side section of pews, so she walked in that direction.

As she stepped into the pew, her uncle stood and gave her a big hug.

"How's my girl? We're glad to have you back in Eden," he added as the two of them sat down, and Willy leaned across him to greet her aunt.

Settling back into the pew, Willy glanced around the congregation. She saw Frank and Eva Gray sitting a few rows ahead of her in the center section. She couldn't stop her thoughts from flitting to Marsh, as she observed that he was not with his parents, not today anyway.

Closing her eyes, she let the organ music wash over her for a few moments. Then, opening them, she gazed at the life-sized mural of Jesus on the wall behind the altar. It had been painted many years before by an itinerant artist who had stayed briefly in the village. Under the mural were lettered the words, *Come Unto Me*. In Willy's opinion, the painting had always been one of the nicest things about the little country church.

The congregation rose to sing the opening hymn,

"Holy, Holy, Holy," and Willy joined in with enthusiasm as the choir filed down the aisle and took their places in the choir loft.

Willy glanced up as she became aware of a person slipping into the pew beside her. She started and gasped as she looked into the green-flecked hazel eyes that were smiling down at her.

"Marsh," she murmured, as she felt the blood drain to her feet, leaving her slightly light-headed.

"Hello, Willy. May I share your hymnal?" he asked as he took hold of the right side of the book.

She nodded and let go with her right hand, letting it drop to her side. *Oh, my,* she thought, as she tried to fight down the butterflies that were madly flapping their wings in her stomach. *Don't panic. It'll be all right.* She took a steadying breath and tried to find her place in the hymn.

Willy stepped a little closer to Uncle Karl so that Marsh would have a little more room, but Marsh simply moved with her. When the hymn ended, they sat down. Willy's knees were shaky.

Wearing a navy blazer over gray trousers, his snow-white shirt accented the tan of his skin, and his eyes picked up the green in his print necktie. *He's even better looking in person,* she thought, *than on television.* She groaned inwardly.

Willy survived the next hour, but she was in a state of agitation and could hardly concentrate on the pastor's sermon. She and Marsh didn't speak again, though he smiled at her several times as they stood and sat, going through the ritual of morning worship.

It felt strange to be sitting there in church beside Marsh, but so familiar too. They weren't talking, but this was the longest time they had actually spent together in ten years. Willy wondered why he had chosen to sit with her today. He could have easily joined his parents in their pew.

Why was she being thrown together with Marsh again? He's married, now. It's not the same as when they were kids. Was there something she didn't know?

Willy surreptitiously glanced at Marsh's left hand where it rested on his thigh. No wedding ring. But, that didn't tell her anything. She hadn't seen him in six years, and he may have never worn one. She sighed and shifted nervously in the pew.

At the end of the service, Marsh greeted Willy's aunt and uncle, then he stepped out into the aisle to allow Willy to precede him out of the church.

At the door, Pastor Ward greeted Willy warmly. Shaking her hand, he said, "Welcome home, Willy. I'd heard that you were to be here for the summer. I saw your mother on Friday."

"It's good to be back in Eden, Pastor, and thank you for your prayer on Mother's behalf. I certainly appreciate it."

"We all wish her a speedy recovery, dear." Then, noticing Marshall behind her, "Good morning, Marsh. It's good to see you here again too. Seems like old times, you and Willy coming through the line together."

"But, we're not—" Willy began, but Marsh urged her forward in the line as he responded to Pastor Ward's greeting.

As they exited the church into the bright sunlight falling onto the wide sidewalk before the building, Willy squinted up at Marsh's handsome face.

"Marsh, I wanted to tell him that we weren't together." She sounded exasperated.

"It's all right, Willy, no harm done. Two old friends can sit together in church, can't they?" he answered with a casual shrug of his shoulders.

"Oh, I suppose so, but I didn't want to give him the wrong impression. Isn't Alicia with you?" Willy added a little caustically as she unknotted her scarf and slipped it off her shoulders.

"No, she isn't," he answered as his left eyebrow arched in surprise. "How do you know her name? I haven't seen you since I married her."

Willy flushed guiltily, but she lifted her chin defiantly and looked him in the eye.

"Your mother writes to me occasionally. She told me."

"That's how I knew you were in Texas too." Marsh grinned disarmingly. His glance flickered over Willy's trim form as he thought how pretty she looked. He added, "Good ole Mom."

"Yes, she's a sweetheart."

"Willy, I'd really like to . . ." Marsh broke off when a group of older ladies descended on Willy to welcome her home.

He stepped away when an old friend of his father's motioned for him to join him. After a few minutes of small talk with Mr. Treon and his young grandson, Marsh excused himself to go back to Willy. Unfortunately, she'd disappeared.

Willy had gone back into the vestibule when she remembered an item in the bulletin requesting volunteers to chaperone a Youth Fellowship outing the next Saturday evening.

This should be fun, she thought as she signed her name. Noting that the leaders were Phil and Vi Dunaway, she wondered if they were Dusti and Jack's parents. Jotting down their phone number on a pad in her purse, she made a mental note to call them later in the week.

Emerging again into the bright sunlight, she saw her aunt and uncle standing near her mother's car. She joined them there.

"We were looking for you, dear. Would you like to come home with us for Sunday dinner? I have chicken roasting in the oven as we speak," Aunt Hilda urged.

"Oh, yes, thank you. That sounds great!"

As Willy drove out of the parking lot to follow her uncle's car to Tulip Lane, she didn't notice Marshall trying to catch her eye from where he had been waylaid by the Dunaway kids.

"What were you saying, Jack?" he asked, turning his attention back to the two youngsters.

"Just that Dusti and I wondered if you'd like to volunteer to be one of the chaperones for our Youth Fellowship's hayride and swimming party at Bradford Lake next Saturday. Mom and Dad will go, but we could use a couple of other grownups along, too," the boy replied eagerly.

"Well, okay, that sounds like fun. It wouldn't hurt to give a little time back, now that I'm one of those grownups," Marsh said pleasantly in reply.

Dusti grinned. "There's a sign-up sheet in the vestibule. Mom and Dad will be glad to have you along."

A few minutes later, Marsh went back into the church. Picking up the pen to sign, he smiled when he saw that Willy had volunteered just ahead of him. Pleased that they were both going on the hayride just like old times, he thought that it could prove interesting. At the very least, he'd perhaps get a chance to ask her to talk with him.

Back in Eden

He smiled as he left the church and walked down the road toward Eden. He took off his navy blazer and loosened his tie. Slinging the jacket over his left shoulder, he glanced up at the clear blue sky. It was a beautiful day, and he felt better than he had in months. He whistled a nameless tune as he strolled along.

Chapter Five

In Aunt Hilda's bright and cheery kitchen, Willy donned an apron over her dress to help with dinner.

"Not too much to do before we can eat, Willy," her aunt said, as she spooned homemade summer relish into a pink glass serving bowl.

"I'll gladly whip the mashed potatoes, Aunt Hilda, if you'll make the gravy. I haven't mastered the art of making good, smooth gravy yet."

"It does take practice," said her aunt, smiling.

"Well, Betsy, who shares my apartment in Katy, and I don't eat it often. Always watching our figures, I guess."

From the dining room door, Uncle Karl joined in with a chuckle.

"As someone said, if you don't watch your figure no one else will!"

Willy laughed and threw a dishtowel at him.

Soon, they were seated at the dining table enjoying the tender roasted chicken with all the trimmings.

Back in Eden

"How is Erich doing at Wright State?" Willy asked, referring to her younger cousin, the Heidlers' only child. "Goodness, this must be his senior year coming up already."

"Yes, it is," Hilda replied, "and he's doing fine. He's working in Dayton this summer, gaining some experience in another area of business."

"That's good. I hope I get to see him this summer."

"Oh, I'm sure you will, Willy. He'll come up to Eden a few times before the summer's over," Karl replied, as he reached for his coffee cup.

"Is he still planning to go to work at the hardware store when he graduates?" Willy asked, laying down her fork and wiping her mouth with her napkin.

"I'm pleased to say that he is," beamed Karl. Looking across the table at his wife, he added, "Mother and I were not sure if that would be the case when he went off to college. We wondered if after being away from Eden for several years, he might want to live and work in a larger town. But, that's not his plan."

Hilda reached across to Karl and squeezed his hand.

"We're both very happy that he wants to join his father in the hardware business. It's good to be able to keep it in the family, and Karl will be able to slow down a bit when Erich comes on board."

"That sounds wonderful. You've been carrying the whole load since Dad died. You deserve a chance to take it easier." Willy smiled at the two of them.

"Erich has some wonderful ideas too, marketing techniques and all that. He'll have our little small town hardware store all modernized before we know it," Karl asserted proudly.

Hilda rose from the table to bring in their dessert, a delicious-looking lemon meringue pie.

"Oh my, Aunt Hilda, that looks so good!" Willy exclaimed. "There goes that figure we were talking about earlier, Uncle Karl."

A little later, after helping wash the dinner dishes, Willy mentioned that she planned to visit her mother that afternoon.

"Would you like to ride along with me?" she asked.

"That would be very nice, dear. I haven't been down for a few days. Since it's Sunday, Karl is free to go too," replied Aunt Hilda as she hung their aprons up on a hook at the end of a counter.

They made the short drive into Piqua and were soon greeting Grace in her hospital room. The visit was a pleasant one, and a little later was enlivened by the arrival of Mary and her two teenagers.

"Hello, Grandma," Brent and Paige said together as they each kissed her from either side of her bed.

"Oh, it's so good to see you, both of you." Grace asked a few questions about camp and their other activities, and her grandchildren launched into a few stories.

Mary chatted with her aunt and uncle, and Willy took the opportunity to slip from the room. She walked down the hall to the nurse's station.

"Excuse me, I'm Willy Heidler, Grace Heidler's daughter, and I noticed that she still seems to be quite warm and flushed. Can you tell me how she's doing?" she asked the efficient looking and attractive brunette nurse who seemed to be in charge.

"Hello, Miss Heidler. Your mother's temperature is still elevated, and a slight cough has developed. The doctor has ordered some tests done. When he knows the results, he'll most likely adjust her medication."

"Is she in any pain, Mrs. Jakes?" Willy asked, noting the nurse's name on her identification badge. "She seemed cheerful when we arrived just a short time ago," Willy added with a concerned frown on her face.

"Her throat is a bit sore, she told us, but we'll make her as comfortable as we can. Dr. Daw will see her again in a few hours and will have the lab results by then."

Willy sighed, "I hope this doesn't slow her recovery. She so hoped to be going home soon, now that I'm home to look after her."

"Yes, she's mentioned that to me. I know that she enjoys visitors, but perhaps you'd cut the visit short today so that she doesn't overtire," Mrs. Jakes gave her a friendly smile as if to soften her words.

"Of course, we'll do that, and thank you, Mrs. Jakes, for the information."

Willy started toward Grace's room, but turned back and asked, "May I call this evening to check on her?"

"Of course. Whoever is on duty will gladly answer any questions."

Willy nodded her thanks and returned to her mother's room.

Putting on a happy smile to mask her concern, she sat down beside Mary and quietly told her of the nurse's suggestion that they not stay long today.

Mary nodded her agreement, stood, and said, "Mom, the kids and I will tell you goodbye now. We don't want to tire you out." She dropped a kiss on her mother's cheek.

"Goodbye, dear. Come back soon."

"We will, Grandma. Be good," Brent said with a grin.

"Bye, Grandma. I love you," added Paige, as she blew a kiss from the door.

After Hilda and Karl had chatted a little longer with Grace, Willy also suggested that the three of them be on their way.

"Time for your nap, Mom. I'll be down to check on you tomorrow." Leaning over, she brushed a kiss to Grace's forehead and whispered, "Love you."

On the road to Eden, Willy told her aunt and uncle what the nurse had said.

"Oh, dear, I hope our visit didn't tire her too much," Hilda said in a fretful tone.

"I'm sure not, Aunt Hilda. I'm going to phone the nurse's station later to see how she's doing."

Willy dropped Hilda and Karl at their house, then drove home. Having put Grace's car into the garage, Willy entered the house by the backdoor, accompanied by the cats.

"Hello, girls. Do you want your supper already? I guess that would be okay."

Willy fed them, then paced around the house for a few minutes. Realizing that she was fretting about her mother, she decided to do something about it. Stopping by the phone in the hallway, she dropped down onto the cushioned bench, checked a number in the phonebook, and dialed.

When she heard a cheery hello coming through the receiver, she greeted her old friend from high school, Sarah Winchell.

"Hi, Sarah. It's Willy."

"Willy!" Sarah squealed in delight. "How are you? And *where* are you?"

Willy laughed in return. "I'm at my mother's, Sarah. I'd love to see you. May I come over this evening?"

"You sure can, Willy. But don't wait until then.

Come over now and have supper with us. Sam is just lighting his barbecue grill, and we'll put on another burger for you."

"Thank you, Sarah. I'd love to, if you're sure it wouldn't be too much trouble?"

"Not at all, and Sam'll be glad to see you too."

"Okay. You talked me into it," Willy said and chuckled. "I'll change my clothes and be over in a half-hour or so. See you then."

"Bye, hon," Sarah said and hung up.

In a happier frame of mind, Willy put the cats back out and took the stairs two at a time. She freshened up in the bathroom, then changed out of the clothes she had worn to church that morning. Tucking a bright red camp shirt into the waistband of a pair of denim culottes, she slipped into her brown sandals.

Grabbing her shoulderbag, she left the house by the front door as she planned to walk over to the Winchells. Within ten minutes, she had turned onto Bluebell Lane, a street of newer houses on the southeast side of the village.

A block further along, Willy pushed open a gate in a white picket fence and carefully latched it behind her. She strolled up to the front door and rang the bell.

It was almost instantly flung open by a pretty young woman in white shorts, sneakers, and a pink tank top. She was of the same age as Willy, but stood a few inches shorter and wore her shiny blond hair in a smooth short cut.

Throwing her arms around Willy in an exhuberant embrace, Sarah Winchell exclaimed, "Oh, it's so good to see you. Come on in, Willy."

"I'm really glad to see you too," Willy replied, returning Sarah's hug. "Your front yard looks so nice. The sod you put in last fall has really taken hold."

As her friend stepped into the foyer, Sarah said, "Yes, it has. Sam and his brother put up the fence this spring. We put a sturdy chainlink type around the backyard to keep Sammy under control," she added, referring to her three-year-old son, "but I'd always wanted a white picket fence, so we built that across the front."

Willy hunkered down to greet Sammy, a solid-looking redhead who had run up behind his mother to peep around her legs.

"Hi, Sammy. How are you?"

"Tell Aunt Willy fine, honey," Sarah said, as she stooped down to his level.

"Fine," the boy replied with a shy grin for his mother's friend. He then ran back through the house to join his father on the patio.

"My, he's certainly grown."

"Uh–huh, but wait till you see Shannon. She's ten months old now. She's napping but will be up soon."

The two old friends walked through a corner of the living room to the kitchen. Seeing Sam on the patio, Willy called a greeting which he returned with a wave of his spatula and a broad smile.

Sarah insisted that Willy take a seat on a wooden stool pulled up to a counter while she went back to preparing a fresh vegetable salad.

"Are you sure I can't help you?" Willy asked.

"Just talk to me, hon. When did you get back to Eden? I had heard that your mom was in the hospital, so I wondered if you'd be in town this summer."

"I got in on Thursday and have been pretty busy since then. Of course, I've spent time with Mom each day and done a little around her place. Had dinner with Mary and John on Friday evening. Went out to dinner last night and to church this morning, and Aunt Hilda and Uncle Karl invited me to Sunday dinner today after church."

"You *have* been busy. We didn't make it to church this morning, or I would have seen you then. Shannon had a restless, fussy night. She's been teething."

"Well, I'm glad she's having a good nap then, for your sake, Sarah, but I can't wait to hold her again. If she'll let me, that is. But tell me how you and Sam have been."

"We're fine. School's out, of course, but Sam is still teaching driver's ed this summer. Between that and his projects around the house, he's been busy. The kids keep me on the go," she replied with a chuckle as she rinsed off a cucumber to slice for the salad.

Just then there was a cry from down the hall. Sarah quickly dried her hands on a kitchen towel.

"Shannon's awake. I'll just be a few minutes."

"Go ahead. I'll slice the cucumber for you."

By the time Willy was finished and had given the salad a toss, Sarah was back carrying on her hip a rosy-cheeked baby who was chewing on a finger.

"Hello, Shannon. Don't you look sweet. What a cute outfit, Sarah," Willy said, admiring the little yellow playsuit with ruffles on the seat. "Do you think she'd let me hold her?"

"Let's give it a try."

Willy held out her arms and the baby smiled and gurgled, then reached out her arms to Willy who gathered her close.

"Oh, she feels so soft and smells so sweet!" she exclaimed as she kissed the little girl on the top of her pale blond hair. Shannon gurgled again, then reached up and tugged at Willy's white beads. Willy worked the little fingers off of the necklace before it could break.

"You look so natural holding her, Willy. You should settle down, get married, and have some babies," Sarah said with a teasing smile.

"Well, I'd like to do that, but since I don't have a husband in my life, I should wait for motherhood, don't you think?" Willy replied with a grin and an eyebrow raised quizzically at her longtime friend.

"That *would* be the best plan," Sarah replied with a giggle, then set the salad bowl and a gravy boat of homemade salad dressing on the kitchen table. "No suitable prospects in Texas? I'm surprised that one of those rugged cowboy types hasn't whisked you away on his horse and rode off into the sunset with you."

She completed setting the table and poured a cup of milk for Sammy.

"No such luck, girl! I did meet a nice man at the hospital though. One of Mom's doctors. He took me out to dinner on Saturday." She smiled in Sarah's direction, over the baby's head, and waited for the reaction she was sure would come.

Sarah set the bowl of applesauce she was carrying down on the table with a clunk.

"Wow! A doctor! Who is he? And you've only been back in town three days. Fast work, babe!"

"He's Dr. Daw's son, another Bill Daw. He's been back in Piqua for a year or so and has gone into practice with his father. Mom introduced us Thursday evening when he was doing rounds."

"Super! Did you have a good time?" Sarah asked, giving her friend a devilish look.

"Yes, very pleasant. He's good company," Willy answered rather nonchalantly.

"Uh-oh, that was too noncommittal. No zing?"

"Well, like I said, he's very nice. I may go out with him again. I was serious, Sarah, when I said I'd like to get married, have a home of my own and a family."

"You do what you think is right for you, Willy, but it'd be a mistake to settle for second best."

She took her daughter from Willy and put her into a high chair, fastening a safety strap around her. Sarah tied a bib on the baby, then turned to Willy.

"Do you know that Marsh is back in Eden?" Sarah closely watched her friend's expression.

Willy bit her lower lip and looked away. Busying her hands with placing the burger buns, catsup, and mustard on the table, she gave a brief reply.

"Yes, I saw him in church this morning."

"Well, it looks like he intends to stay on here. Sam ran into him at Gilardi's about two weeks ago. He's bought the old Brown place."

Willy's head jerked up, and she glanced quickly at Sarah. "He—he has?" She willed her hands to stop trembling and jammed them into the pockets of her culottes.

"The Brown place. I was just there yesterday. I mean, I was taking a hike around town and ended up walking through the woods there. I—I knew I was trespassing, but I didn't know that Marsh now owned the farm." Willy felt her face warm.

"It's okay, Willy. He probably didn't know you were there, and he wouldn't have minded if he had. You and he were good friends when you were younger."

Willy pressed her hands to her hot cheeks. The look she gave Sarah was pure pain.

"Oh, Willy, I'm sorry. I didn't realize. You still have feelings for him, don't you? I wasn't sure as you hadn't mentioned him for years." Sarah crossed the kitchen and hugged her. "Don't worry. I'm the only one who knows how crazy about him you were in high school. He treated you like a little sister, but I always suspected that his feelings ran a little deeper than that."

Willy returned the hug, then pulled away as Sam and Sammy came to the patio door and slid it open.

"Are we ready to eat, ladies? These burgers are perfectly done, if we do say so ourselves. Right, Sammy?" his father asked, as he set the platter at the end of the table. The little boy giggled, and Sam tousled his hair affectionately before turning to Willy.

"How are you, Willy? You look great." Sam, also a solid-looking redhead, a much larger version of his son, smiled warmly at her.

"I'm good, Sam, thank you. Sarah has been telling me how busy you both have been," she replied as she forced herself to relax and put Marsh from her mind.

In a short time they were seated around the table.

"We haven't bought a patio table yet, so we'll have to have our meal inside," Sarah explained. "With getting the yard in shape and putting in the fencing, well, money only stretches so far."

"Inside is fine with me. I think your home is just lovely."

"Thanks, Willy," Sam said with a smile. "There are a lot of things to do yet. We've started a small vegetable garden this year and plan to add some dwarf fruit trees in the fall." His voice carried the unmistakable tone of a proud new homeowner.

Sarah added, "We were lucky that the lot already had those two mature maples at the west edge. They give us some nice shade of an afternoon for the backyard."

The pleasant meal in the company of an old friend and her family was just what Willy needed to put her into a better frame of mind. She answered their questions about the latest happenings at Katy and her mother's illness.

When Sam brought up Marshall's name near the end of the meal, Willy was able to remain calm. Sam and Marsh had been good friends in school and in the same graduating class, so it was natural for him to mention his being back in Eden.

"Did Sarah tell you that Marsh has bought the Brown farm? I ran into him not long ago at the grocery, and we had a nice talk."

"Yes, I told her," his wife interjected, as she spooned the last bite of applesauce from Shannon's dish into the baby's tiny mouth.

Willy took a deep breath, then asked Sam, "How is Marsh?"

She used her napkin, then folded her hands in her lap and awaited his reply.

"He looked good. Well, maybe a little tired, but he passed that off as stress. He said his wife wasn't with him, but didn't elaborate. I didn't want to pry."

Willy said, "I saw him at church this morning. In fact, he came in a little late and slipped into the pew beside me where I was sitting with Aunt Hilda and Uncle Karl. It surprised me that he'd do that as it's been years since I've even seen him, let alone talked to him. Since well before he got married." She finished with a jerky little smile aimed in Sarah's general direction.

Sarah turned to Willy. "Really? I didn't realize you'd sat with him. What did he have to say? Did you get a chance to talk?"

"No, not really. It was a strange feeling to sit there with him again, singing the old hymns. Outside, I asked about Alicia, and he was surprised that I knew her name. I was a little embarrassed to admit that his mother writes to me a couple times a year and that she had told me." She paused and sipped her lemonade.

"But he just grinned and said that that was how he knew I was teaching in Texas. He was about to say more, but someone interrupted us. I left with Hilda and Karl soon after that."

"Hm-mm," murmured Sarah. "Alicia isn't with him, and he's been here for several months. I wonder if they've split or are in the process?"

"I couldn't say," her husband stated, as he rose from the table. Bringing a damp cloth from the sink, he wiped Sammy's mouth and hands. "All done, big guy? Let's visit the bathroom," he added, as he lifted the boy down from his stool.

Following his son from the room, he turned back to the women still at the table.

"By the way, I asked Marsh to join us for dinner sometime soon. If you could be here too, Willy, we could all have a nice visit."

Willy looked at Sarah in a bit of a panic as Sam left the room.

"I'm not sure I can do that, Sarah. He's married, and we don't really know if they've separated. Remembering how Marsh felt about commitment, I can't see him divorcing his wife."

Her friend reached across the table and patted her hand.

"But there can be circumstances under which anyone may change their minds about something like that. We don't know if they've been happy. How long have they been together?"

Willy replied, "About three years, I think. There was a child on the way once. Mrs. Gray told me that Alicia had miscarried early in the pregnancy and that Marsh was very disappointed." Willy sat and worried her paper napkin in her hands.

"Don't fret, hon. Since Sam brought up having Marsh to dinner, of course I'll ask him, but you don't have to be here unless you want to be."

She used the damp cloth and tidied the baby's face and fingers. "You know, Willy, nothing would make me happier than you and Marsh getting together."

"I gave up on that when he married, but I still think about him a lot, too much for my peace of mind." Willy grimaced. "I've never told you this, old friend, but he kissed me once, and I've never been able to forget it. I'm afraid I compare any other man's kiss to that one. It's foolish of me, I know, but I can't seem to help it."

"Remember what I said earlier about not settling for second best?" Sarah said earnestly. "That'd be a mistake you'd probably regret forever." Then, conspiratorially, she added, "We just have to find out if he *is* divorced and take it from there. I'd love to have you living back in Eden again, Willy."

"I'd like that too, in fact, I was thinking of looking for a teaching position for the fall, either in Eden or close by. I feel that Mom shouldn't be living alone anymore, and if I were here, it would take some of the pressure off Mary too. And, this was *before* I even knew Marsh was back," she added defensively.

Sarah smiled, her blue eyes lighting up in pleasure. "You are? That's wonderful news."

Sam and his son returned to the kitchen just as Sarah spoke.

"What wonderful news, Sarah?" he asked.

"Willy has been thinking of looking for a job in Eden for next school year to be close to her mother again. Isn't that great?" his wife replied with enthusiasm.

"Sure is. Let's see, you've been teaching history in Texas, right?"

"Yes, American history and government classes, plus advising the FTA group and assistant coaching the girls' soccer team."

Sam, who taught chemistry and physics classes at Eden High, said, "Well, the scuttlebutt has it that Gloria Rokita is expecting again. If that's the case, she may want out of her contract for next year. Currently, she's teaching Ohio history in the eighth grades and American history in the upper grades."

By way of explanation to Willy, Sarah added, "Gloria and her husband dearly want a family, but she has trouble carrying to full term. She's miscarried twice now. She told me at a faculty party last Christmas that if she was fortunate enough to get pregnant again, she would most likely have to have complete bed rest. If she's expecting, I suspect she won't be able to teach next year."

"Do you suppose I should put my name in right

Back in Eden

away, Sam?" Willy asked, a little spurt of excitement bringing a sparkle to her eyes.

"Yes, call the superintendent tomorrow. He's new to you, Ted Dunbar, but I'm sure you'd like him. He's fair and sensible in his dealings with both the students and the faculty."

Willy smiled at the two of them, and baby Shannon giggled in response as Willy patted her head.

"I'll do that tomorrow, Sam. If there's a chance to be hired here, I want to take care of it quickly as I'll have to let the Katy School District know as soon as possible. Only fair to them, and then Betsy, my roommate needs to know too."

After helping Sarah tidy the kitchen and load the dishwasher, they visited in the living room for awhile. Willy took her leave of the Winchells well before dark, explaining to them that she planned to call the hospital that evening.

"Thanks so much for a lovely meal and your good company," Willy said warmly as she hugged Sarah goodbye.

"I'll be talking to you soon," Sarah responded.

Sam added, "Let us know what Ted Dunbar says, Willy."

Back at the house on Sycamore Street, Willy put in the call to the hospital, and when she asked, was put through to the nurse's station on third floor north.

"Nurse's station," said a crisp business-like female voice. "Miss Burnside here."

Willy quickly identified herself and asked about her mother's condition. There was a pause while the nurse pulled out the Heidler chart.

To Willy's surprise, a male voice came on the line.

"Willy, this is Bill. I had just returned Grace's chart to the station. When I realized it was you on the phone, I thought I'd take the call."

"Oh, hello, Bill. Thank you for doing that. How is she? The nurse on duty this afternoon said you'd know more by this evening after the lab work was complete."

"Yes, she's picked up a virus which has elevated her temperature again. Of course, that also plays havoc with her blood sugar levels and slows down the healing process with the foot ulcer. We've changed her medication and will keep a close watch on her."

"Oh, Bill, I hate to hear this. Is she very uncomfortable?"

"No, at least she isn't complaining, but I've a feeling she doesn't do that often. We'll make her as comfortable as possible, and hopefully this will pass in a few days."

"May I visit her tomorrow?"

"It would be better not to, Willy. She needs a lot of rest, and she'll understand why you can't come. You don't want to catch the virus. Unfortunately, it's not uncommon for a patient, while their resistance is low, to pick up another bug while hospitalized. I'm sorry."

"Me, too," Willy replied, sounding depressed. "Thanks, Bill, for taking such good care of her and for letting me know."

"You're welcome. If all goes well, I'd still like to join you next Friday evening for the dance."

"Yes, if all goes well, I'll see you then. Bye, Bill."

"Goodnight, Willy."

Hanging up the phone, Willy sat dejectedly on the phonebench in the hall.

"Pooh, I wish this hadn't happened."

Picking up the phone again, Willy put in a quick call to Mary and then to Hilda to fill them in on what had happened. Then, she climbed the stairs and started to get ready for bed.

Stopping after removing her make-up and brushing her teeth, she put on a pair of black running shorts and a white T-shirt instead of her pajamas. Returning to the bathroom, she grabbed a towel from the shelf and went down to the kitchen, where she filled a small water bottle. Putting it and her house key in her fanny pack, she headed out the door.

It was too early to go to bed, and she was too restless to just sit around. Since it wasn't completely dark yet, there was time to run some laps around the track.

Walking down Main Street, Willy soon came to the schoolgrounds. She followed the path that led down into the natural bowl. Placing her towel and fanny pack on a bleacher seat, Willy did a few stretches and began to jog.

By the time Willy completed two laps, she felt better. This was what she had needed, some real exercise to lower her stress level. She had felt good when she got back to Eden, other than the worry about her mother, but the old stress had elevated again. She felt it was seeing Marsh this morning, then talking about him tonight, plus she couldn't seem to keep him out of her thoughts and dreams of late.

Ten years ago, she could have walked up to him and asked him anything and he would have given her an honest answer. But since that day in the woods, everything had changed. For years, she could hardly talk around him, let alone ask him why it had happened. She was sure it had meant nothing to him; it was just an aberration, never to be repeated.

It hadn't been repeated either. In fact, today in church was the longest time they had spent together since that day. Willy had been surprised and nervous, but it hadn't been as uncomfortable as she'd have thought. Not quite, but almost like the old days. With one big exception: he was married now. *Or was he?*

Willy was halfway through her third lap when she noticed a movement ahead of her near the edge of Eden Road where it dipped down from the schoolhouse hill to meet Main Street. Her heart skipped a beat and she almost lost her stride as a glimmer of fear flashed down her spine.

Dusk was falling fast, but the remaining light was enough to allow her to make out a tall man wearing a white shirt and dark pants. He walked down the slope and neared the track. He waved at about the same time Willy realized it was Marsh. The fear faded with that recognition, but her heartbeat went into overdrive as he neared her.

Marshall had walked down Schoolhouse Hill and started down the slope to the track when he spotted a runner coming toward him. The white shirt stood out in the gathering dusk. There was something familiar about that stride and form. He recognized Willy at about the same time she saw him, if that little break in her stride was any indication. He hoped he hadn't frightened her. Marsh waved, then walked toward her as she neared the curve in the track.

"Hi," he said. He matched his stride to hers as he joined her on the track.

"Hi," she replied as she tried to get her breathing back under control.

They jogged another lap in silence. Willy was a little apprehensive at first, but she soon became more attuned to Marsh's presence. It began to feel like the old days.

As they neared their starting point, he said, "Once more around for old times' sake?" She knew he was thinking of the old days too.

"To the bleachers," she replied a little breathlessly.

Slowing the pace as she neared the bleachers, Willy did some stretches to cool down. She'd run a bit more than a mile. Wiping her face, neck and arms on her towel, she offered it to Marsh who took it and used it. She then shared a drink of her water with him.

"Thanks, Willy," he said as he handed the bottle back to her. She took another sip before returning it to her fanny pack.

"I hope I didn't frighten you appearing so suddenly like that."

"You did give me a start before I recognized you. I wasn't expecting anyone to be around."

"I've been jogging a few laps each evening, then taking a walk through town before going home. I seem to sleep better if I do that."

Willy looked up into his handsome face. He looked tired, as Sam had said. She hadn't noticed it this morning at church.

Aloud, she said, "That's why I came down tonight. I was feeling upset and knew I wouldn't sleep if I went straight to bed."

"What's wrong, if you don't mind my asking?"

Chapter Six

Willy fought back the hot tears she felt just behind her eyelids.

"Several things, Marsh, but mostly Mom. She's in the hospital because of her diabetes, and now she's caught a virus to boot. She's why I'm home now, though I probably would've visited later in the summer." Her words trailed off when she realized how trembly her voice sounded.

"I'm sorry she's ill, Willy. Come on," he urged, "let me walk you home."

"Oh, no, Marsh, that's not necessary," she protested and turned away from him. That old skittishness had come back, and she felt the need to put some distance between them.

"Please, I'd like to talk with you. I wanted to this morning after church, but there wasn't a good opportunity. Perhaps we could talk now at your house?" He gave her one of his most winning smiles, and she felt a sinking feeling.

She knew she'd not be able to say no. She sighed, picked up her fanny pack, and fastened it on.

From around his waist, he untied a zippered sweatjacket that matched the navy of his pants and dropped it around her shoulders.

"It's cooling down. Don't want you getting chilled."

Willy pulled it a bit closer and looked up. He was looking back at her with such tenderness and concern that a lump formed in her throat. She couldn't speak. He hadn't changed that much, still the big brother looking after his little sister. She let out a shaky sigh.

He turned to the path that led up and out of the bowl. She followed, and they walked silently toward Sycamore Street, both lost in their own thoughts.

When they reached the Heidler house, Willy unlocked the front door and they stepped inside. She unfastened her fanny pack and dropped it on a hall table where she turned on a lamp, then slipped Marsh's jacket from her shoulders.

Handing it to him, she said, "Thanks, Marsh, for the use of your jacket and for the walk home."

"You're welcome, but I *do* want to talk. May I stay a little while?" He looked around and seemed to make a decision. "May we sit on the porch swing, Willy?"

She hesitated for a moment. "Well, all right. Let me get a jacket." She lifted a light windbreaker from a coatrack in the hall. Marsh put on his sweatjacket and pushed open the screen door, allowing her to go ahead of him.

Willy sat at one end of the swing, Marsh at the other. He laid his right arm across the back of the swing behind her but not touching her. Willy sat quietly, her hands clasped in her lap while Marsh set the swing into a gentle swaying motion with his left foot.

He rested his right foot on his left knee and grasped his ankle with his left hand.

This is crazy, Willy thought. They'd sat out here so many times, years ago, and she'd always felt very comfortable talking with him. Now she couldn't seem to form a sensible thought, let alone say it aloud. She wondered what he was thinking.

She stole a glance at him. In the dim light that spilled onto the porch through the screen door, she could see that his eyes were closed. He looked so— so at ease, and she was a jumble of nerves. She took a steadying breath and asked for help in saying the right thing.

Marsh broke the silence.

"It's been so many years, too many, since we sat on this swing and talked. I always enjoyed those talks, Willy. I've missed them, and I've missed you."

Willy could hardly believe what she was hearing, and she stammered a little.

"I enjoyed those talks, too, and I—I've missed you, Marsh. When we grew apart, I was very sad for a long time."

Marsh turned slightly so that he could see her face.

"It made you sad? I'm sorry, Willy. I apologize for the hurt I must have caused you. I never meant to do that. Some time I hope we can talk about that day. You were so special to me, and I treated you terribly. It's laid heavy on my heart ever since. Can you forgive me, please?"

"Oh, Marsh," Willy pressed her hands to her mouth and squeezed her eyes shut, making an unsuccessful effort to keep the tears from escaping. Her voice unsteady, she answered, "I'm so sorry too. I was hurt, but I must've hurt you too. When I'd see you after that, I never knew what to say or do, and so I'd just avoid you as much as possible."

"Yes, I thought that was what you were doing. I didn't blame you, but I cared so much about you, little sis, even though you could be a pest at times," he teased. "We're older now. We should be able to talk and laugh again." He raised his left hand and brushed away a few of her tears. "Please, don't cry, Willy. If I'm not careful, I'll be crying too."

Willy sniffed and dug in her shorts pocket. Finding a tissue, she wiped her face and blew her nose.

"I've never seen you cry, Marsh," she said on a little hiccup.

"No, you haven't, but I've done my share these past ten years."

"Hard to believe that it's been ten years," Willy said as she loudly blew her nose again.

Marsh moved his right hand onto her right shoulder, giving it a little squeeze. She was glad the cloth of the windbreaker was a barrier between her skin and his touch. She heard his low chuckle.

"Willy, for such a sweet little girl, you always could make like a foghorn when you blew your nose."

Some of her tension eased and she laughed in return as she said, "Me? Marsh, you've always been such a tease."

"I always loved teasing you; you'd get so indignant and angry with me. Sometimes you'd actually sputter!" Marsh laughed harder at the memory.

Willy sniffed again. "I loved your teasing, even though I'd complain about it," she admitted. "I think I've missed it." She looked away from him and down at her hands which were wadding her damp tissue into a tiny ball.

Marsh pulled her a little closer and laid her head on his right shoulder. "Willy, I'm glad that you've missed it—and me."

Willy let herself relax a little against him, even though a little niggling voice arose inside her and cautioned that she shouldn't.

His voice low, Marsh said, "I saw Mrs. Harper on her porch when we got here. Do you suppose she's still there?"

"Probably," Willy murmured back, "and probably disapproving."

Marsh chuckled, "Maybe if I keep the swing moving, she'll not think too badly of us."

"Yes, she's sure to hear these creaking chains and know that we're just swinging."

Marsh tensed. He dropped a quick kiss to the top of her head, then abruptly stood. Willy felt her scalp tingle.

"Sorry, Willy, I wasn't thinking how this would look to an outsider," he said, and leaned back against the porch railing, resting his weight on his hands on either side of his body.

She folded her arms across her stomach and seemed to draw into herself. "Yes, for a second there, I forgot you're married now," she replied with a catch in her low voice.

Willy thought she'd never seen such a look of pain on his face in all the years she'd known him. It twisted at her heart.

"We—we don't have to talk about it, Marsh. I can see it upsets you."

"I need to, Willy. I want to tell you that the marriage fell apart. About five months ago, before I moved back to Eden, Alicia and I divorced, though she took her sweet time agreeing to it." A hint of bitterness crept into his quiet voice.

Willy leaned forward. "Are you sure that's what you want? You've always felt so strongly about commitment, Marsh, it surprises me to hear this."

Marsh gave a harsh laugh. "I know, Willy. I guess I was rather idealistic as a teenager, wasn't I?"

"Perhaps you could still work it out with her. She may still love you." Willy thought, *how could any woman not love him?*

"No, there's no chance of that." He ran his hands through his short hair and sighed. "I think I need to tell someone about it. I haven't wanted to burden my folks with the unpleasant details, but—well, do you mind, Willy?" His look cut straight to her heart.

"Of course not. I'll listen." She knew it would hurt to hear it, but he obviously needed to talk about it. She steeled herself to listen to his words, no matter what the cost to her emotionally.

There was a loud purr from out of the darkness and Cleo leaped onto the porch rail, walking along it to Marsh's left hand. He petted her, then lifted her to his chest and cradled the friendly cat in his arms.

"Well, hello, old girl," he murmured as he stroked her back with one hand. Cleo gave another longer purr of pure contentment, and Marsh looked across her to Willy where she sat on the swing watching him.

"I met Alicia my third year of law school," he began slowly. "I'd never dated much in college, too busy, I suppose, and I think I'd left my heart . . . never mind." He looked down at Cleo and frowned.

Willy's heart skipped a beat at those words. *What did he mean?* She whispered, "Please, go on."

"I worked as a clerk in her father's law firm that

last year of school. I met her there. She was around a lot, and she was very beautiful. I guess it turned my head to have her pay so much attention to me. Anyway, we started dating."

He paused and turned away from her. Looking out over the Heidler yard, he said in a rather jerky voice, "We married, and her father took me into his law firm. It didn't go well from the beginning, but I'm not making excuses." Cleo, seeming to sense his agitation, leaped back onto the rail, walked a few feet away, and began an evening bath.

Marsh drew a deep breath and continued, "Alicia became pregnant almost right away. At first I was a bit panicked, but I quickly changed my mind and started looking forward to the baby.

"Then, a few weeks later, I came home one day to find her in bed. She told me she hadn't felt well and had gone to the doctor. She'd miscarried while in his office; he'd examined her and told her to go home and stay in bed and rest for a few days. She assured me that she'd be all right."

Willy groaned his name. Standing, she touched his arm to urge him to turn to face her.

"I'm so sorry. To lose your baby—it must've been terrible. I can't imagine how I would've felt in your place. But, surely Alicia was also upset."

Marsh's face contorted in anguish.

"Please, sit down again. Tell me what happened?"

They sat down on the swing. Marsh was quiet for several minutes. When he spoke, it was in a low, controlled voice, as if he were holding in all emotion. Willy's heart hurt to hear it.

"Over the next year or two, I suggested several times that we try again to have a child. She knew that

I wanted a family, but she refused to even consider it. After awhile, I stopped even suggesting it as we'd always have a real row over it."

Willy asked quietly, "Was the issue of a baby the only reason for the separation, Marsh?"

"No." He continued, "It wasn't long before I realized that Alicia didn't really want the same things I did. Getting started in my career, I was very busy but making a good living. Alicia didn't seem to mind. She still enjoyed her friends and social life, much of it without me, and she relished being hostess at all the functions her father's firm put on or attending them with him."

He paused, then laughed derisively at himself.

"I sound jealous, don't I? But, it wasn't that way at all. I tired of the type of cases I was assigned. Rich clients, divorces, child custody battles, getting people out of messes they shouldn't have gotten into in the first place, if only they'd used good sense and not depended on their money to solve the problem for them." Marsh spoke more animatedly, and Willy sensed the passion he had always felt for the law overriding the earlier pain.

She said, "That doesn't sound like the career you'd always talked about. When did you decide to join Bertram Jones in his practice?"

Marsh looked at her in surprise. "How did you know about that, Willy?"

"Oh, just about everyone I've seen since I got in from Katy last Thursday has mentioned it to me," she answered with a little smile. "Like my brother-in-law John, Aunt Hilda, Sarah and Sam."

"Oh, yeah, I did run into John and Sam recently. But to answer your question, last Christmas when I came up to visit the folks, I met old Bert for lunch. He told me that he really wanted to slow down, take a younger man on. You know, I've wanted to work in the areas that he has all these years."

She smiled warmly, "Yes, I remember your visits to his office back in high school. I've always felt his influence turned you toward studying law."

"You're right. And when he asked me to join him, I couldn't have been happier. But back in Cincinnati, the news was not welcomed, believe me. Alicia hit the ceiling. No way was she going to leave her society friends and father and the city to live up here. You would've thought I'd suggested moving to Antarctica. She never has even pretended to like Eden or my parents."

"But, not like your folks? Everyone loves them!" Willy could not contain her disbelief.

Marsh leaned forward, his elbows resting on his knees, his hands hanging loosely, and seemed lost in his private thoughts. Willy waited patiently, knowing that all this baring of his soul had to be hard. He had always been proud, even as a boy.

Finally, he straightened and began to gently sway the porch swing again. Willy still waited. The last few years had been very difficult for him. She had had no idea.

"When I told her I had looked at a farm I wanted to buy up here, it was the final straw to her. I'd be the first to admit that Alicia was not at all the person I thought she was when I married her, but this woman was a complete stranger to me. She threw a tantrum, cursing and raging at me, throwing things across the room and at me, and she said something—at first I thought I must have misunderstood her, but I hadn't. She repeated it, loud and clear."

He stood abruptly and leaned again on the porchrail, staring out toward the street.

Willy stood also, and followed him. Putting her left hand between his shoulderblades, she massaged the tense cords there. "Marsh? If you don't want to say any more, it's okay. I'm just so sorry that all this has happened to you," she murmured soothingly.

"Thanks." Marsh straightened and brushed a hand across his eyes. He spoke in a strained voice. "Willy, this is the hardest part for me to forgive. She screamed at me that I'd been so easy to fool; she laughed and said that many of the times she'd been out 'with her father' or 'with her girlfriends' were only excuses. She'd been seeing other men for months."

Willy flinched and bit her lower lip. Her voice shaky, she groaned, "Oh, no, Marsh."

After a few minutes, Marsh took a long, shuddering breath. "I'm sorry to lay this on you, Willy, but thanks for listening to me. My male pride's hurt, I suppose. I went into that marriage in good faith. I'd never have done that to her. Why was it so easy for her to run around on me?"

Willy answered in an anguished voice, "I can't begin to speak for her, but there are just some people—both men and women—who don't live by the same values as most of us. There are just no words to express how sad this makes me feel. I'm sorry for Alicia. Someday she may regret what she did very much."

"Perhaps," Marsh said, though he didn't sound as if he believed it. "Things were already pretty bad between us, but when she told me that . . . well, despite the committment I'd made, I knew I couldn't stay married to her. It would have been a complete sham."

"So you started divorce proceedings and moved back to Eden," Willy concluded.

"Yes, I think it's been the wisest move I've made in a very long time."

Willy looked away for a moment. "I'm glad you confided in me, Marsh. I certainly understand now why you've made such a change in your life. Talking with you again feels good."

Marsh smiled a little grimly and rubbed the back of his neck with his right hand.

"I know I feel better for telling you about what happened, Willy. Thanks again for listening, It's getting late and I should head home. I hope the word on your mother is good tomorrow. Give her my best wishes, please."

"I will, thank you." As he turned to go, she added, almost as an afterthought, "Are you staying with your folks or at the Brown place? Rather, I guess it's your place now."

Marsh smiled, "At first, with them, but I needed some time alone to think things through. I catch a meal with them pretty often, but I've been bedding down in my old sleeping bag for awhile. Maybe—that is, if you'd like to—you'll come by soon. I'd like to show you the work I've done on the house."

Willy returned his smile. He sounded better now that they'd talked. *That's good,* she thought. "I'd like that. Does the house still have those lovely bay windows front and back? And the gazebo in the yard?" Her interest and curiosity showed in her pretty face.

"Sure does," he replied as he thought how ten years hadn't changed her that much. *She's still a sweet, bright, compassionate young woman who loves people and life.* He looked at her for a minute and added, "This'll be a busy week for me, but I hope to see you later on. Perhaps we can go jogging again?"

She laughed and it sounded like a chorus of angels to his ears. "Perhaps we'll run into each other at the track some evening."

"Sounds good." Marsh hesitated, then stepped toward her. "Goodnight, Willy," he whispered and kissed her cheek. "Thank you for being here, and for just being you."

Willy stood very still, her hand to her cheek where he had just brushed his lips. "Goodnight," was all she could manage to say. She watched him walk down the driveway to the street, her heart pounding in her ears.

Stepping inside, Willy closed and automatically locked the door, hung up her jacket, picked up her fanny pack, turned off the lamp, and walked upstairs. Going through the ritual of preparing for bed, she took a quick shower, and was soon in bed. All the while, her mind digested what Marsh had told her.

A sympathetic tear escaped down one cheek. Alicia had hurt Marsh so much. She hoped that speaking of it tonight helped him, but what happened might not be easy to lay to rest, she realized. *Please, Lord, help him find the peace of mind he needs.* Willy understood Marsh's seeking a divorce now. He was still the honest, high–principled young man she'd known and loved years ago. *Yes, I loved him then, and to be honest, I love him still, but is there a future for us? Dare I hope for one?*

Willy closed her eyes. Feeling drained by the emotional events of the day, she fell into a restless sleep.

* * *

Up early on Monday morning, Willy did her laundry and pressed a few things. Shortly after nine o'clock, she called the office of the high school and arranged a meeting with Mr. Dunbar, as Sam had suggested.

Later in the morning, she phoned the nurse's station to check on her mother and learned that she'd had a restless night. The nurse on duty felt that the new medication would bring an improvement before the day was over. Willy asked her to tell her mother that, since Dr. Daw had suggested she not go in today, she would phone her mother's room late in the afternoon to talk to her directly.

Thanking the nurse, Willy hung up the phone. A little worry line etched her forehead, even though she was sure they were doing all they could to help her mother.

After an early lunch, Willy freshened up and changed into her newly cleaned cream suit that she'd worn on the plane. She gave her appearance one last check in the hall mirror and glanced at her wristwatch. It was time to leave for her one o'clock appointment at the school complex.

It had been a few years since Willy had been in the high school. She took the opportunity to look around the corridors. Not too much had changed. School buildings were so strangely quiet when the students weren't there—almost eerily quiet. She smiled at her own mystical imagination.

Willy turned in the direction of the school offices. Introducing herself to his secretary, Mrs. Meyer, with whom she had spoken earlier in the day, she was shown into the superintendent's pine-paneled office.

Ted Dunbar, a graying slender man in his early fifties, welcomed her, giving her a firm handshake. "Have a seat, Ms. Heidler," he said and sat down behind his cluttered desk. She did so, taking one of the two green padded chairs opposite him.

Willy told him a little of her connection with Eden and the fact that she had been thinking of returning to the area permanently.

"My friend Sarah is married to Sam Winchell, and when I spoke of this, he suggested that I contact you immediately."

"Ah, yes, Sam. A fine young teacher. Has a good rapport with his students."

"Having grown up in Eden, I've known Sam and Sarah for many years. He thought there may be an opening in your social studies department for the fall, though he did say it was only a rumor. As that's my field, I wanted to talk with you about that possibility."

"As a matter of fact, I did receive a resignation just last week. A happy one, as Mrs. Rokita is expecting a baby. But she won't be able to fulfill her contract for next school year. Tell me more about yourself, Ms. Heidler, your training and teaching experience."

He and Willy talked for the next half hour. She answered his questions, and he informed her of what would be expected of her if she should be offered the position. They also exchanged their philosphies of teaching; not too dissimilar, considering the difference in their ages.

Concluding the interview, Mr. Dunbar asked her to complete a formal application in the outer office. "Mrs. Meyer will have the forms there," he said. "I'm pleased that you came in today, Ms. Heidler. There's a school board meeting this evening, and I'll present your application to them. I should have an answer by this time next week."

"Wonderful," she replied, "and thank you for seeing me and for considering me for the opening."

With another firm shake of his hand, Willy returned to the outer office and accepted the application forms from the secretary. Completing them within the half hour, she said goodbye and left the school.

Chapter Seven

About four-thirty in the afternoon, when she thought Grace would be awake from her nap but not yet served her dinner, Willy called directly into her room.

"Hello, Mom, it's Willy. How do you feel?"

"Hello, dear. A little better," her mother replied, though her voice sounded scratchy. "The new medicine seems to be working on this bug."

"Good. I'm sorry I couldn't come in today as I have a lot to tell you, but Bill, Young Doc, suggested that the family not visit for a few days. Give you a chance to rest and to keep any of us from getting the same virus."

"Yes, he said the same to me, dear. I missed you today, but it's for the best. What did you have to tell me?"

"A couple of things, Mom. I had supper with Sarah and Sam last evening and learned of an opening on the staff at Eden High. Sam recommended that I see

Mr. Dunbar about it, and so I phoned for an appointment this morning. I saw him this afternoon, and it looks promising, Mom, though I won't know for sure for a week."

"Oh, my! That's exciting news, but are you sure you want to move back to Eden? I know you enjoy your job in Katy."

"I've been thinking about it for some time, and when I got back to Eden this time, well, it felt so much like what I needed in my life. I really enjoy the small town atmosphere and being around old friends and neighbors. I guess I'm an Eden girl at heart. Aunt Hilda said it best. She suggested that if my *heart* were here, perhaps I should be too." Willy took a deep breath.

"If this is truly what you want, it'd make me very happy. Just don't make a change for my sake. I wouldn't want that, though I'd love having you here again," Grace added in a trembling voice.

"Now, don't cry, Mom. I've missed you too, and of course it's not definite as yet. The other thing is that I've seen Marsh, twice actually. He came in a little late to church yesterday and sat with me, Aunt Hilda, and Uncle Karl. It surprised me, as he could've sat with Frank and Eva, but he didn't. That was the longest time I've spent with him since he left for college, even though we only spoke briefly. I was nervous, Mom. I think you know why, but it wasn't as uncomfortable as it could've been, I suppose."

"Karl told me yesterday that he'd heard that Marsh had bought the old Brown farm. It seems that he's back in Eden for good," Grace said.

"Yes, he's joining Bertram Jones in his practice. In

fact, he's been working with him for a few months now."

Willy paused, then continued, "Mom, remember saying that perhaps Marsh and I should talk while we're both in Eden? Well, we have. It's not all cleared away yet, but we made a start. I went down to the schoolgrounds to jog on the track last night, and he came down to do the same and joined me for a couple of laps, then walked me home. We sat out on the porch swing and talked, just like we did so often years ago. It felt awkward at first, but I managed to relax a bit as we talked."

"Did he explain why he's making a change in his life, Willy?" her mother asked.

"Yes, we talked at length about it. His marriage has been very troubled, Mom. Something happened a few months ago that led to his asking Alicia for a divorce. I asked and he said that there's absolutely no chance of a reconciliation, and I believe him, Mom. He's still upset by what happened, and I feel really bad for him."

"Willy," her mother started to talk, then stopped to clear her throat. "Willy, please be careful. I know you care very deeply for him, but his emotions have to be in turmoil at this time. He may not know what he really wants yet."

Willy hesitated before assuring her mother that she understood her concern, but not to worry. "I'll talk with him again if he wants. I think I can be a friend, as he seems to need one right now. I spent a lot of time thinking and praying about the situation since we talked. Dad always said to trust in the Lord and you can't go wrong."

She could almost feel her mother's smile down the

phoneline as she said, "Yes, dear, you do that, and I'll be praying for you and Marshall too."

"Thanks, I love you, Mom. I'd better hang up and let you save your voice. I'll phone again tomorrow and be in to see you when your doctors will allow. Goodnight."

" 'Night, sweetheart."

The rest of the week went by swiftly. Willy kept busy with the house, garden, and yardwork, and found time to take Paige to lunch and to visit some other friends. She joined Sarah on a shopping excursion to Harris Mills. She soon agreed with the young mother that two adults were better than one when it came to handling two children in a crowded shopping mall, but Willy thoroughly enjoyed the trip. She also took the opportunity to share with Sarah that Marsh was definitely divorced, though she wasn't free to say why.

Willy went to the track to jog a few laps each evening and enjoyed the exercise. She was disappointed not to run into Marsh, but supposed he was too busy elsewhere.

Young Doc phoned on Thursday evening to tell her that Grace could begin having visitors again. She thanked him, and he confirmed that he still planned to come up to Eden for the dance on Friday.

So, on Friday afternoon, Willy drove into Piqua and spent an enjoyable hour catching up with her mother. She was thrilled to see Grace looking and sounding so much better.

"I do feel better and happy to say that I'm not contagious any longer. Dr. Daw won't let me pin him down as to when I can go home though," Grace added.

"It'll be soon now, I'm sure. I'll be glad to have you there."

In response to her mother's question, Willy told her that she hadn't seen Marsh again that week, but told her of her other activities.

"Oh, I nearly forgot," Willy stated, opening her purse and retrieving several paperbacks. "These came in the mail yesterday. I thought you might appreciate something new to read."

Grace, an avid reader and a volunteer at Eden's small local library, expressed her thanks. "Oh, good! My favorite romance writer's latest novel was included in this shipment. I always enjoy Betty Neels' stories." Grace placed the books on her nightstand.

"I'm looking forward to tonight," Willy said with a smile. "There's a dance at the Eden Community Hall. It's a fundraiser for the fire department and emergency squad. Young Doc and I are going to attend. I haven't danced for ages, and Bill says that he hasn't either, so we'll both be pretty rusty," she added laughingly.

Grace smiled, "Well, have a good time there, and say hello to everyone for me."

Willy left the hospital soon thereafter and drove back to Eden. Upon entering the house, she remembered that she had meant to call Vi Dunaway about the Youth Fellowship hayride earlier, so she placed the call.

"Hello, Mrs. Dunaway. This is Willy Heidler. I signed up to help chaperone Saturday's hayride. Is there anything I should bring or know beforehand?"

"Hi, Ms. Heidler. I saw your name on the list, and the kids told me they'd met you while fishing the other day. Welcome back to town," the lady said graciously.

"Thanks, and please call me Willy. I enjoyed meeting Jack and Dusti too."

"And I'm Vi. As to what to bring, just a moment while I check the list. The YF will pay for the soft drinks out of their fund, but some of the parents are donating other items. Would you bring another package of hot dogs and buns? We probably can't have too many of them," she added with a chuckle that any parent of a teenager would understand.

"I'll be glad to. We're leaving from the church at six, right?"

"Yes, Jonas Smith is driving his farm truck for us, and we'll have an hour or so of swimtime at the lake before we eat."

"Oh, dear, I don't think I brought a swimsuit with me this summer. Never mind, it'll be a good excuse to go into Piqua and shop for a new one." Willy laughed and Mrs. Dunaway joined her. "Thank you, Vi. I'll see you tomorrow evening."

"I'll look forward to it. Goodbye."

Willy hadn't even planned to go swimming that summer. In fact, the summer seemed to be full of surprises already, and it'd only just begun. *Hm-mm, didn't someone use that for a song title?* Willy grinned and began humming the tune on her way to the kitchen to fix a quick supper.

When Bill pulled into the driveway a few minutes after eight, Willy was ready. She wore a bright yellow sleeveless sundress with a square neckline edged by a white collar that set off her light tan. It was fitted at the waist with a flared skirt ending just below the knee, just right for dancing. On her feet she wore comfortable white flats.

Back in Eden

Bill looked relaxed and casual in navy slacks and a blue and white striped cotton shirt.

"Hi, Bill. Are you ready to dance? We may be rusty, but I bet we'll have fun." She flashed a happy smile as she stepped out onto the porch and walked toward his car.

"Hello, Willy. The fun part sounds good, though there's no maybe about it. I *know* I'm rusty!" he grinned in return.

After the very short drive to the Eden Community Hall, they walked through the open double doors into a small anteroom. Tonight, the larger room was being used as a dance hall.

Karl Heidler was taking donations in the anteroom. Beside him there was a hand-painted sign that reminded one and all to give generously to help the Eden Volunteer Fire Department purchase a second and larger watertank truck.

"Welcome to the dance," he said, smiling broadly.

Willy gave him a kiss on the cheek and returned his smile.

"Hi. Uncle Karl, this is Bill Daw from Piqua, one of Mom's doctors. Bill, meet Karl Heidler."

The two men shook hands and Bill said, "Happy to meet you, sir," to the older gentleman.

"Same here. I hope the two of you have a good time tonight."

"Well, I've warned Willy that my dancing is a little rusty," Bill replied as he reached into his wallet to add a twenty to the growing pile in Karl's wicker basket.

Willy grinned teasingly as she added a bill from her purse. "If I suffer any injury, I'll expect free medical care."

Laughing, Bill retorted, "Okay, that's a deal."

Entering the main room, Willy and Bill stopped to look around. A large space had been cleared for dancing. At the far end, a sound system was set up to amplify the music, which would be mostly tapes and records, but old Mr. Smith and his son, Jonas, were tuning up their fiddles for the square-dancing. Paul Anfinson was just calling the couples forward to set up two squares.

Willy saw Sarah and Sam stand up from one of the round tables arranged in the near end of the room. She waved and caught Sarah's eye, and she and Bill threaded through the tables toward them.

Willy quickly introduced her friends to Bill.

Sarah suggested they join them at their table and also in the set for square-dancing.

Willy glanced up at Bill, leaving the decision to him.

"Thanks," he replied, "but may I sit this first one out and just watch? I've never square-danced, and maybe I can pick up a few pointers if that's okay with you, Willy?"

"Sure. We'll try it later. Go ahead, you two, grab a place in that set."

She and Bill sat down at the table. Paul, the caller, began his lead-in to the first set of the evening. Willy's toes were soon tapping to the lively tune played by the two fiddlers.

"What do you think, Bill? Doesn't it look like fun?"

"Well, yes, but a little complicated."

"Not really—you just follow the caller, and once you get through the first set of patterns, it's just repetition after that." She smiled encouragingly at him. "I'll help you get it right."

"Okay, I'm game. We'll try the next one."

Back in Eden 117

When Sarah and Sam came back to the table, the four of them chatted while Bill became acquainted with Willy's old friends.

When the music for a slow dance started, both couples took to the dance floor.

A few minutes into the dance, Willy smiled up at Bill and said, "You're not so rusty. Not one bruised toe yet."

"You're lucky. I'm concentrating really hard." He smiled in return and twirled her around, much to her delight.

So, when the next square dance set was called, they joined Sarah and Sam as half the set. The other two couples were Jack Dunaway and a pretty brunette girl he quickly introduced as Jeannie Marlowe, and a forty-ish couple who turned out to be Jack's parents, Vi and Phil.

After a few stumbles and missteps, Bill caught on to what the caller's cues meant, and before long was having a good time, as were the others.

Returning to their table, Bill rolled his shirt cuffs up his forearms.

"Whew!" said Sarah as she fanned her face with her hand. "Fun, but warm."

Sam and Bill excused themselves to go for some cool drinks, and Sarah took the opportunity to comment on how nice Bill appeared to be.

"It's almost a shame that there's no spark, Willy," she added in a low tone for Willy's ears alone.

"That's true. He's a really fine man and fun too. But I have to be fair to him," she replied, also in an undertone.

The men returned with colas for all and paper-lined baskets of popcorn and pretzels to share.

"Thanks, guys," both girls said as they took a sip of their drinks.

After they had cooled down, Bill asked Willy to dance to a slow number that was just starting. Agreeing, they were soon on the dance floor swaying to a romantic old standard.

"Good of them to turn the lights down for these slow numbers," Bill commented, bending his head a little to speak into Willy's ear.

"Uh-huh. Nicer, and more people will get up and dance that way. Less embarrassing if you don't feel that you're a very good dancer," she replied quietly. "Of course, it's a bit more romantic too."

"That's probably their *real* intention."

She felt the tickle of Bill's breath as he chuckled near her ear, and she smiled. As Bill turned her a little as they danced, she caught her own breath and tensed briefly as she looked over Bill's shoulder and met a pair of sober greenish-hazel eyes.

When did Marsh come in? she asked herself. *And how long has he been watching Bill and me dance?*

"What is it, Willy?" Bill asked quietly, obviously noticing her sudden reaction.

"Oh, nothing, Bill. An old friend just came in is all. I was surprised to see him here," she replied. That was true, but it sounded like a lame excuse. *Oh, well.*

Marsh stood there, tall and dark in black slacks and a dark green polo shirt open at the throat. She found she couldn't look away. Then he casually moved among the tables, nodding and speaking to people. Willy saw him spot Sam and Sarah, and he joined them at their table.

She took a deep steadying breath and decided there was no reason to be concerned. She would simply introduce Bill to him casually and it'd be no problem at all. But her mind raced. *Why did he look so intensely at us? It almost felt like that time years ago when he watched Jerry Ellison and me dance.*

Willy felt Bill's hand at the small of her back guiding her as they walked across the dance floor. She put a bright smile on her face as they neared the table. Marshall stood as they approached.

"Hello, Marsh. Let me introduce you to Bill Daw from Piqua. Bill, this is Marshall Gray, an old friend of mine who's recently moved back to Eden." She sat down and caught Sarah's eye, giving her a look that screamed, *help!*

The two men shook hands across the table and sat down. Sarah launched into small talk meant to put everyone, especially Willy, at ease. When Sam asked Willy if she had spoken with Ted Dunbar, she replied in the affirmative, which led to a short explanation of her plans to perhaps stay in Eden.

"Of course, it's too soon to know if I'll be hired for next year, but there's an opening in my area," she added, taking a sip of her drink.

"If they're smart, they'll snap you up," Marsh said, flashing a grin across the table at her.

"Thanks for the vote of confidence. Too bad you're not on the school board," she joked back.

"So, you may be here past the summer. That's good to hear." Bill reached for a pretzel and then bit down on it.

Sarah chose that moment to ask Willy to join her in a visit to the ladies room, and the two of them escaped.

"Wow," Sarah said, breathing a sigh of relief as she closed the door behind them. "Marsh was so tense when he first stopped at our table. Sam and I had seen him come in, and he had zeroed right in on you and Bill dancing. We asked him to join us, but didn't tell him you and Bill were sitting there too. Probably a little mean of us."

"I saw him watching us. Actually, I'm glad I saw him. It gave me a chance to gather my wits before we came back to the table," Willy answered from one of the stalls.

"Sure would like to know what's going on in his mind," Sarah said as she washed her hands at a sink. "Maybe Sam will get an idea if we let the three of them talk alone for a bit," she added mischievously.

"Sarah, you little devil!" Willy laughed aloud at her friend's duplicity. "But in a way I'm surprised that Marsh came tonight, by himself, I mean," she added more seriously.

"Oh, nothing unusual in that. All ages, married and single, come to these community dances. Besides, it's for a good cause."

Willy ran a comb through her fluffy hair and said, "Well, old girl, shall we re-enter the fray?"

"Ready. Don't want to leave three good-looking males alone *too* long," Sarah laughed as she followed Willy out the door.

Back at the table, they found the Dunaway kids talking with Marsh and the others. Dusti sat on the extra chair, and Jack leaned on her chairback.

"Hi, again, Miss Heidler, and Mrs. Winchell," said Dusti.

"Hello, Dusti; hi, Jack," both ladies answered.

"Are you two having a good time?" Willy asked, as she sat down beside Bill.

"Super!" replied Jack. "Say, Miss Heidler, do you

think I could have the next dance?" he added with a hopeful look on his young face.

"Of course, Jack, that would be very nice," Willy replied without a moment's hesitation, rising from her chair. "Excuse me, Bill."

Marsh said, "I haven't danced a single step tonight. Dusti, would you do me the honor?" He stood and bowed to the young girl, who blushed prettily as she stood also and took his offered hand. "Now, mind you, Miss Dunaway, I tend to have two left feet," he added with a grin as they stepped away from the table.

Sam called to the teenager, "Don't believe him, Dusti. He was the best dancer in our class in school."

The next dance was a two-step which Willy and Jack got right into with no hesitation.

"Jack, you're a very good dancer. Where did you learn?"

"Mom taught me mostly. She says all guys should learn to dance as girls appreciate a good dancer." He gave her a big grin.

"She's right. Girls do, and grownup women do too." She returned his smile and glanced around. "Dusti and Marsh look like they're having a good time."

"Dusti likes to dance, and she thinks Marsh is *dreamy*," Jack stated, wrinkling his nose a little as he imitated Dusti's higher voice on that last word.

Willy laughed, "Do you tease your little sister a lot, Jack? Silly question, of course you do. I remember that a lot of girls thought Marshall Gray was dreamy in high school."

"Gee, did you, Miss Heidler?"

"Afraid so, Jack, but he and I never dated."

"Hey, if I'd've been him, I would've asked you

out." The expression on his face was so earnest that Willy stifled the giggle that arose in her throat.

"Why, thank you, that's a very nice compliment."

The boy grinned and looked embarrassed at what he had just said.

After another half-turn around the floor, Paul, at the microphone, announced that this was a tag dance.

"When I say change partners, the guys tag the shoulder of the gal to his right. Ready? Change partners!"

Willy felt a tag and turned to find Uncle Karl beaming at her, as Jack moved on to partner Carrie Mills who had been dancing with her husband, Steve.

"It's been a long time since I danced with my favorite niece," her uncle said as they got back into step.

"It certainly has, Uncle Karl."

"This is a little quicker step than I usually try. I'm more of a shuffler, but Hilda loves to dance, you know."

"I'm glad to see you out dancing. That's what I like about these community dances. All ages come to them and have fun together."

A minute or so later, Paul called, "Ready? Change partners."

Karl moved on to Carrie, and Willy felt a hand touch her shoulder. The little jolt of anticipation that went through her told her it was Marsh before she even turned. She raised her hands and moved into his arms, smiling in response to the twinkle in his gorgeous eyes.

"Hello again. I was hoping I'd get to dance with you, but I wasn't sure if I should ask, since you're here with a date."

"I don't believe Bill would mind. Besides, my being

at a dance with a date never stopped you from asking before," she added, flashing a beautiful smile.

Marsh chuckled low in his throat. "Willy Heidler, I believe you just flirted with me."

"Oh, my, I *do* apologize, sir," she replied in a fluttery voice. Scarlett O'Hara would have been proud.

"Don't apologize. Just between you and me, I loved it."

Willy's heart was beating faster, and she had a feeling it had nothing to do with the quick two-step they were dancing.

She looked up and caught a devilish gleam in his expressive eyes, dark green in the dimmer light.

"Now you're teasing *me,* Marsh."

"Maybe. Maybe not. All those times I've teased you, Willy, it was always done with the utmost affection."

"With—with the utmost affection?" She stammered a little over the words. *Pooh,* she thought, her spirits sinking, *not love, just the utmost affection. Well, what did I expect? Always the reliable big brother.* She couldn't quite stifle a regretful sigh.

As the music ended, she stepped back a little. Marsh still held one of her hands.

"One more dance, for old times' sake, Willy? We always did dance well together," he asked quietly.

"Yes, we always did. All right, Marsh. It's been a long time, hasn't it?"

"Too long," he agreed as he swung her into a slower dance to an old country-western tune. He positioned her just a little to the right of him, both facing forward. She placed her left hand in his left, and her right over his right hand where it rested on her shoulder. They moved in perfect unison as if all those years hadn't gone by.

Step, slide, step, slide, pause, first to the left, then to the right and back again to the left. Marsh lifted her left hand and she turned under it to face him. His right hand touched her waist and she twirled back to her original position, with her hand over his on her shoulder.

Following the other dancers as they made a large circle of the dance floor, Willy thought, *I don't want this to end.*

But end it did. Marsh gave her one last twirl, then slipped his right hand behind her back and with a flourish dipped her. Holding her in that position for a moment, he looked deeply into her dark brown eyes which were wide with surprise. She couldn't help it and convulsed in giggles. He lifted her back onto both feet, laughing himself.

"You never could do a dip seriously, Willy, you always broke up laughing!"

"I know. I'm terrible, but it always does that to me. That was great, dancing those old steps again. Thanks for asking, Marsh."

"My pleasure, Willy," he said, and they walked off the dance floor hand in hand. When they reached the tables, he released her hand and guided her ahead of him.

As they sat down, Bill observed dryly that he didn't think that was the first time they'd danced together.

Sam laughingly retorted, "These two always did cut a mean rug together. Even entered a few contests, if I remember correctly."

Willy smiled around the table. "But we never won."

"Came close a few times," commented Marsh, and he took a sip of his cola.

As a new song came over the speakers, Sarah grabbed her husband's hand and pulled him to his feet.

"Our turn, Sam, I love to dance to this one."

"Okay, hon," he replied. "Excuse us, everyone."

"Shall we have another go, Willy?" asked Bill, as he stood and reached for the back of her chair.

"Sure. Excuse us, Marsh."

"Mm-hm. I think I'll circulate. Maybe I'll find someone willing to square-dance the next set with me," he answered.

Chapter Eight

True to his word, when Paul called for dancers to form two new sets, Marsh joined their square with Marie Treon, a pretty blond woman in her mid-twenties.

Willy felt a pang of jealousy but tried to squelch it. *Be nice,* she told herself. Willy knew that Marie was single. *Is Marsh interested in her?*

Willy gritted her teeth but smiled. She hoped no one could tell how she really felt as she moved through the dance.

Marie accompanied Marsh back to their table and he introduced her to Bill, as, of course, Willy and the others already knew her.

"Marie, this is Bill Daw, a doctor from Piqua. Bill, Marie Treon, who is a registered nurse on staff at Loramie General. I thought you should meet each other," Marsh added with a guileless smile and maneuvered Marie into a chair beside Bill.

Willy couldn't believe it. She glanced across the

table and met Sarah's twinkling eyes. Her friend looked as if she were going to lose it any moment, and Sam was no better, as he was looking up at the ceiling with a big grin on his face. Marsh looked exceedingly pleased with himself. *What's he up to?* Willy thought. She gritted her teeth again, but this time was tempted to give Marsh a swift kick under the table.

A few minutes later, when Paul announced he was putting on Glenn Miller's "In the Mood" and called for all the die-hard jitterbugs to get out onto the dance floor, Marsh said, "Come on, Willy, this'll be fun!"

She briefly hesitated, but couldn't resist the sparkle in his eyes, so she took his hand and said, "Sure." Turning to Bill, she said, "Excuse us."

He glanced at her, and said, "Hm? Oh, sure, Willy," and went back to his conversation with Marie.

Sarah said to Sam, "Let's see what we can remember, hon."

Sam groaned, but got up to follow her to the dance floor.

By this time, Marsh had led Willy there also and stopped at the edge to remove his loafers.

"Take your shoes off, Willy. We can move better in just our socks."

Willy started to protest, but instead laughingly shook her head in disbelief and stepped out of her flats, placing them alongside Marsh's shoes.

A moment later, he was snapping his fingers to get into the rhythm and off they went. Willy hadn't danced so hard or enjoyed anything so much in years. *Funny how it all came back, and how easy it still was to follow his moves,* she thought as she twirled and spun out and back to his arms. As the last notes faded out, she twirled into him one last time, and he held her there in a bear hug.

The onlookers applauded the half-dozen couples of all ages who had braved Paul's call to jitterbug.

"You haven't lost a bit of your style, Marsh. That was so much fun! I haven't danced myself breathless like this in years."

He released his hold. "I haven't felt like dancing at all in years. Thanks, Willy. I'm glad I decided to come tonight. I was at Gilardi's and saw the poster on the bulletin board earlier tonight. Agnes almost insisted that I come to the dance. She said you never know who'll be there."

Willy smiled, "Agnes said the same thing to me a few days ago. I think I should tell her thank you."

"Me too."

They were still there on the dance floor when the lights lowered and a new song began. Marsh said in a coaxing tone, "It's been years since you and I danced to this tune. May I, Willy?" He gently pulled her back into his arms.

"I'm not sure." She glanced toward Bill, who was deep in conversation with the lovely Marie.

"Bill won't mind."

She made a little face. "I don't think he even knows I'm gone. Did you do that on purpose? Bring Marie over to our table, I mean." She looked up at him accusingly as they started to move to the popular tune from their high school days.

"Guilty as charged, your honor," he replied, grinning down at her.

"He's really a very nice man," she said, frowning at him.

"I'm sure he is, Willy, but he's not for you."

"Marshall Gray," she began indignantly, "you certainly have a nerve."

"Now, now, don't get all bent out of shape, little sis."

Exasperated, she snapped, "Really, Marsh, he's just a new friend. I only met him a week or so ago. Anyway, if he's not for me, who is? In your esteemed opinion, that is." Her eyes flashed with the anger she was not bothering to hide.

Suddenly sober, he replied, "You'll know one of these days, Willy." He looked deeply into her dark eyes which widened in amazement. *Goodness,* she thought, as a tremor went through her. He snuggled her a little closer and laid his cheek just above her right temple. "Relax, Willy, it's okay," he murmured soothingly.

She took a steadying breath. Forcing herself to concentrate on the music and the slow steps, she gradually felt more in control.

"Hmm, you smell so nice. I remember that fragrance; it always made me think of spring," Marsh spoke quietly near her ear, then lifted his head to look into her pretty face.

Willy smiled, "That's probably because it's lilac, and thank you."

Feeling grateful that he didn't know quite how much he affected her, the scent of a spicy aftershave assailed her. She put a bit more space between them.

Willy was almost glad when the song ended and they made their way back to their table. Sam and Sarah had just sat down too, having stayed on to dance to the old song.

Sam said, "We'd better be heading home. Told our sitter we'd be back by eleven-thirty."

"It's been a fun evening. Glad to have met you, Bill, and good to see you again, Marie. Bye, Marsh. Call me tomorrow, Willy. Okay?" added Sarah.

"I should go too. I've a bathroom awaiting a paintbrush tomorrow, and I promised to chaperone a hayride in the evening," Marsh said with a grimace. "Hope I'm up to *that* challenge."

Willy looked at him sharply. "You're going on the YF hayride? I signed up last Sunday at church to do that too."

"Well, hey, I'll pick you up a little before six. No sense in both of us driving over to the church," Marsh offered, speaking nonchalantly.

"I guess that would be all right," Willy replied. Then, a little more graciously, "Fine, thanks, Marsh."

Marie said goodnight to everyone and went to find her brother and sister-in-law with whom she had come to the dance.

"Are you ready to leave too, Bill?" his date asked.

"Whenever you are, Willy," he agreed, standing to pull out her chair. "Goodnight, Marsh, glad to have met you." He shook his hand, reaching behind Willy's back, then added, "It's been interesting."

Willy didn't see the smile the two men exchanged.

"Life in Eden has always been interesting to say the least," Marsh stated a little cryptically.

What did he mean by that? Willy turned and her eyes followed Marsh as he left them and walked to the door.

Pulling into the Heidler driveway, Bill turned off the engine and sat behind the wheel for a minute or so. Willy looked at him questioningly.

"Thank you, Bill, for a fun evening. You were a good sport to tackle square-dancing."

He turned a little toward her. "I enjoyed it once I got started. I enjoyed meeting your friends tonight too. I take it you, Marsh, and the Winchells go back a long way?"

Relaxing back in her seat, Willy said, "Yes, we do. We went through school together. Sarah was my best girlfriend in those growing up years."

"And was Marsh your best boyfriend?" Bill asked, keeping his voice neutral.

"Why no, Bill." Surprise showing in her voice, she went on, "He and I were good friends, but we never dated. He treated me like a kid sister."

Bill lapsed into silence and slipped his right arm behind her onto the seatback.

Willy couldn't decide where this conversation was headed, so she asked, "Bill, what is it? Is something wrong?"

He smiled wryly. "No, not really. I'm going to be frank with you, Willy. I don't think you know how much Marsh cares for you. Perhaps he doesn't know himself yet."

Willy looked sharply up at him, half turning in the bucket seat.

"You must be mistaken! Marsh has just been divorced. I'm sure he's not interested in getting involved again so soon, but—" She paused and looked down at her hands, which were twisting the strap of her purse. "Why do you think that, Bill?" she added in a small voice.

He took her chin firmly in his left hand to turn her face to his. "A man can often tell when another man is interested in a woman. I could read him pretty well, but he keeps you from seeing it, Willy. I believe Sam and Sarah are aware of it too. But what cinched it for me was his bringing Marie over especially to introduce her." Bill chuckled low in his throat.

Willy looked a little puzzled. "I wondered at the time why he did that. Sam and Sarah seemed to think it was awfully funny."

"See? I told you that they knew." Bill grinned at her and released her chin.

Willy's answering smile trembled as she said, "You've been straight with me, Bill. I owe you the same. I care very deeply for Marsh, and have for as long as I can remember, but I've been trying not to let my heart rule my head. Tonight I did seem to be getting mixed signals from him. It's been six years since we've seen one another, and during that time I've tried to put him out of my mind."

"But you can't, can you?" Bill touched his lips to her forehead. "You're a one-man woman, Willy. It's just my bad luck that I'm not the man. I'm still glad we met, though, but I'm going to draw back because it's obvious to me that you and he love each other."

Tears glistening in her eyes, she whispered, "You're a wonderful man, Bill. I'm glad we met too, and I'm probably a fool for not falling in love with you."

"Maybe," he said ruefully, "but I have a good feeling about you and Marsh. I expect an invitation to the wedding one of these days."

He opened his car door. "I'm going to escort you to your castle door now, fair maiden, and make sure there are no dragons lurking about, then tell you goodnight."

Willy smiled and took his offered hand when he opened her door, bowing low.

"Oh, noble knight, you honor me with your kind deeds and solicitations," she murmured as she curtsied in response to his courtly bow.

On the porch, she tiptoed to kiss his cheek, and he embraced her warmly.

"Goodnight, Bill. Thanks again for what has been a surprising evening."

"You're welcome, Willy, and I'll be seeing you."

She unlocked the door, and he started to leave. With one foot on the steps, he turned back to her.

"You know, Willy, Marsh did do me a nice turn when he introduced me to Marie. You wouldn't mind if I asked her out, would you?" His face had an expectant look, almost boyish in its intensity.

Willy's voice was warm with affection as she replied, "I think it'd be very nice if you did. She's lovely, and you have a lot in common. I think you *should* ask her out."

She laughed, a clear, happy sound on the night air. "You have my blessing, noble knight."

Bill chuckled, stepped forward, took her hand in his, and kissed it.

"This humble knight thanks thee, fair maiden."

By nine the next morning, Willy was at Gilardi's. She bought the hot dogs and buns she needed for the hayride that evening and a few things to stock the cupboards at her mother's house.

"Good morning, Agnes," she said cheerily to the fixture behind the checkout counter. "I went to the dance last night as you suggested, and I really did have a nice time."

"Hi, Willy. Good, I'm glad you went. Did you find plenty of willing dance partners?" she asked as she efficiently scanned the product labels of Willy's groceries.

"Uh-huh. Actually, a friend from Piqua went with me. Bill Daw, one of Mom's doctors."

"Oh my, a doctor! I'm impressed," the lady fanned her face with one hand, feigning breathless amazement, then chuckled merrily.

Willy laughed in return. "He's just a good friend, Agnes, but a very nice one. Sam and Sarah were there too, and Marsh came in a little later."

"I'm glad to hear that. He's been back in Eden for several months now, and from what I can tell, hasn't been doing anything but working hard. Both at his job and fixing up that old house he bought. Had to have been good for him to see old friends and dance a bit."

"Well, we certainly did that. He dragged me out onto the floor to jitterbug and nearly danced me off my feet. He's still a great dancer. He mentioned that you had urged him to go to the dance." Willy gathered up her bags of groceries and grinned impishly. "Thanks, Agnes."

"You're very welcome, Willy, and not just for the groceries." The lady gave her a wink.

Willy laughed as she went out the door into the sunshine of a gorgeous June day.

Back home, she checked through the dresser and chest of drawers in her bedroom on the chance that she had left an old swimsuit there. In the depths of the bottom drawer in the chest she found one.

Laughing to herself, she wondered if it still fit. Quickly shedding her shorts and tank top, she tried on the two-piece suit.

"Hey, not bad, old girl! In fact, I think you fill it

out better than at age fourteen," she said to her reflection in the mirror. *Hardly a surprise.*

Singing "Itsy bitsy, teeny weeny, yellow polka dot bikini," she ran downstairs to the hall phone to dial Sarah's number.

"Hi, Sarah. Guess what I found in a drawer in my room? Remember the yellow polka dot bikinis we bought years ago?"

"Oh, my goodness! I sure do, in fact, I still have mine too. I'm pleased to say that I can still get into it," her friend answered proudly, then laughed merrily.

"Congratulations, old girl! I'm duly impressed, and after two babies too. I fill mine out a bit better than I did at fourteen, but it still fits well enough," Willy replied with a giggle.

"Remember wearing them at Bradford Lake that day? The guys hooted at us and sang that crazy song as we walked by."

"Yep, I was just singing it myself as I ran down the stairs. We were so embarrassed and pretended to pay no attention to them, if I recall," Willy said.

Sarah laughed as she said in agreement, "Then we never wore them in public again! Only for sunbathing in our own backyards."

"I guess I'll have to shop for a suit in Piqua today," Willy inserted, "as I sure can't wear this bikini. I didn't bring one with me this trip, and there'll be swimming before the wiener roast tonight."

"Speaking of Marsh," Sarah began.

"Oh," Willy interrupted, "I didn't know we were?"

Sarah joined Willy's laugh and went on. "I wanted to relay what Sam told me after we got home last night."

Willy had to admit that her interest was piqued.

"Go on, Sarah."

"Okay, since you asked," Sarah replied haughtily. "Sam said when you and I went to the ladies room, those two talked together, finding out about one another and how long each had known you. He said something like two roosters ruffling their feathers, but being very polite to each other. Sam thought it was very funny, but also said he thought they actually liked each other."

"From what Bill said when he took me home, they did, at least he likes Marsh." Willy continued, "We had a nice talk. The short of it is that he's pulling back, as he can see that I love Marsh, and he thinks Marsh loves me."

Sarah gasped in surprise. "Really? Sam thought that Bill would pursue you big time with Marsh in the picture."

"I admitted that I care very much for Marsh, and I told him of Marsh's situation right now and that he's always treated me like a sister. Bill said that he could generally tell when a man's interested in a woman, and Marsh shows all the signs. Odd, though. Bill thinks Marsh deliberately hides it from me."

"That may be so, hon," Sarah replied thoughtfully, "he may not feel free to speak of it yet, or he may not be sure at this point exactly how he feels toward you. Getting a divorce may have him a little unsure of himself."

Willy agreed that Sarah may well be right. Marsh was at a turning point in his life. There was a lot on his plate just now—changing his career, remodeling his house, settling into a new life in Eden. He wouldn't make a change in their relationship until he was sure he was over his ex-wife. If he wanted to change it, that is.

"I'm just not sure how he feels, but that's probably true, Sarah. At least one good thing came from the evening. Bill appreciated Marsh introducing him to Marie, and he even asked if it was okay with me if he asked her out. Bill is so sweet. Of course, I said it was fine."

"Well, what do you know? It certainly turned out to be an interesting evening, didn't it?"

"You said it! Well, I'd better get myself together and drive into Piqua. I'll check on Mom and shop for a new swimsuit. Something proper for a high school teacher to wear around kids who *may* be her students next year."

"Yes," Sarah agreed cheerily, "no yellow bikinis! Bye, and have fun tonight."

"Bye, Sarah, and thanks for the talk."

Within the hour, Willy drove into Piqua and stopped first at her mother's hospital room. She found Grace sitting in a chair alongside her bed with her injured foot propped on a pillow on a stool.

"Hi, Mom. It's nice to see you out of that bed. How are you feeling?"

"Much better, dear. I'm glad to be out of that bed for a few minutes too," she replied as she hugged Willy, who had stooped to kiss her cheek.

"I know I'm here a little earlier than usual, but I need to shop for a swimsuit for tonight. In case I have trouble finding one that's right, I wanted to give myself plenty of time." Willy dropped onto the chair near her mother.

"A swimsuit? Where are you going tonight?" Grace asked curiously.

"Well, I volunteered to help chaperone a YF hayride this evening, then learned later that it involved a swimming party too." She grinned and made a little grimace. "I should've remembered that from the old days. Anyway, I didn't bring a suit with me this summer."

Grace looked thoughtful. "Hm-mm, have you checked your room? There may be an old one tucked away somewhere."

Willy grinned. "Yes, I did and found one, but it was that yellow polka dot bikini. Remember when Sarah and I bought them?"

"Oh my, yes," her mother answered, pressing both her hands to her mouth and chuckling. "Your father and I didn't exactly approve of your choice that time, but we decided it would be a waste of breath to say so."

"I called Sarah this morning, and we had a good laugh over them too. We wore them just one time, and then kept them for sunbathing in the backyard *only*. Anyway, I think I'd better shop for something more conservative to wear tonight as a chaperone for a group of teenagers, don't you?"

Grace reached over and patted her hand. "Yes, dear, definitely."

They spent the next half-hour reminiscing about other funny events and scrapes Willy and Sarah had gotten themselves into over the years.

Willy also told Grace a little about the dance the previous evening, but not everything. She felt the need to hold her feelings about dancing with Marsh again inside for awhile.

Back in Eden

When Grace's lunch was served, Willy excused herself to go do her shopping.

"Have fun this evening, Willy."

"I'll try my best, Mom. See you tomorrow," she added with a wave from the door.

Willy stopped at a small shop on Main Street where she had often found clothing to her liking in years past. No such luck this time as most of the swimwear on display was of a skimpy two-piece style. Willy had a definite type of suit in mind, and another bikini was not it. She drove to the mall on the east side of the city where she knew she'd have a variety of women's clothing stores to check out.

Willy stood in the changing room of the fifth store she'd tried. Tugging at the bottom of a one-piece suit, she turned to see it from all angles. A frown creased her forehead. It was black, but not as sedate as she had hoped to find. Everything she had tried on seemed to be backless or cut too low in front or too high in the legs. This one seemed to be the best choice so far. She sighed as she tugged the front up an inch.

Actually, she observed, she looked pretty good. If it were for around the pool at the apartment complex in Katy, she wouldn't hesitate. Glancing at her wristwatch, she groaned. She'd been at this nearly three hours already. *Okay, enough, this one would have to do.* Peeling off the spandex, she quickly donned her shorts and shirt. Selecting a small vinyl beachbag from a rack, she paid for her purchases and headed for the car.

Willy heard the light rap on the front door from where she stood at a counter in the kitchen.

"Just a moment, Marsh," she called, as she placed the packages of hot dogs and buns into a plastic grocery bag. Walking down the hall, Willy told him to come on in, which he did.

"Hi, Willy. All ready to go?"

"Just about. I guess I'll take these hot dogs as they are. I imagine Vi Dunaway will have a cooler to put them in until later." She spoke rather quickly, not really sure of what she was saying. The sight of Marsh in well-worn jeans, an old Eden High sweatshirt, and baseball cap had taken her back to their high school days. Pulling her eyes from him with an effort, she bent to pick up her things from the hall phonebench.

"Probably," Marsh answered rather distractedly as he watched her movements. He took a deep breath. "Here, let me help you with that."

"Okay," she agreed. He took her blanket and sweatshirt from the bench and they went out onto the porch. Willy pulled the door locked behind her.

Marsh opened the passenger door of a nearly new white Toyota pickup and Willy hopped in. Placing her two bags at her feet, she relieved Marsh of the blanket and shirt and piled them on top of his blanket already in the middle of the benchseat.

"Nice truck," she said as Marsh got behind the wheel.

"Thanks. I got it when I moved back to Eden." He smiled rather sheepishly. "I succumbed to temptation and drove a little red sports car while I worked in Cincinnati, but this seems more practical for here. It allows me to haul things that I need to work on the house." Starting the truck, he backed out of the driveway.

Remembering what he'd said about the house last

weekend, she said, "I'll have to stop over to see your progress one of these days."

"Yes. I got the downstairs bath painted as planned today, and the refrigerator and range were delivered this week, so things are slowly coming along." He glanced her way. "Why not tomorrow?"

"Why not tomorrow what?" she asked vaguely. Mentally, she chastised herself. She concentrated to keep him from seeing how being around him bothered her.

Marsh raised an eyebrow at her and grinned. *Not like Willy to be so spacey.* Aloud he answered, "Tomorrow would be a good day to see the house. It's Sunday, and I'll be around all day."

"Fine. We'll do that."

"We're here, Willy," Marsh said as she sat unmoving.

"Oh, yes." She hurriedly released her seatbelt, opened her door, and stepped down to the ground.

Marsh gathered the blankets and her sweatshirt into one arm, and Willy picked up her beachbag and sack of food. "Does this bag come with us too?" she asked, as Marsh came around to her side of the truck.

"Yes, when I called Vi Dunaway, she told me to bring them. I'm the Marshmallow Man tonight."

"Good." Willy looked up at him. "A wiener roast without toasted marshmallows would be a total disaster." *That's better,* she told herself, *keep it very casual, and don't think any personal thoughts about him.*

Vi hailed them from across the church parking lot and they walked over to her. She had a cooler sitting on the tailgate of a station wagon. Willy gave her the hot dogs which she placed inside, then took the buns and marshmallows to stow in a cardboard box.

Just then, Jonas Smith pulled into the lot in his farm truck. Marsh piled the rest of their things into Willy's waiting arms and took the cooler over to the truck cab followed by Vi with the box of dry food items. Willy trailed behind.

"Good evening, Jonas," Marsh said.

"Evening, Marshall," the older man replied as he helped fit the things into the space. "A good night for a hayride."

"Yes, a fine night," Marsh said with a smile. "Something about going on a hayride makes me feel young again."

Jonas and Vi both laughed. "Shucks, boy, you *are* young!" the man added.

Phil Dunaway walked up with the cooler of soft drinks to add to the other containers. He said, "Well, I guess we can begin loading the back of the truck now."

Marsh went to the back and climbed agilely up and over the closed tailgate. Willy handed up the blankets, her beachbag, and Marsh's sack holding his swimtrunks and towel. Pausing to pull her old Miami University sweatshirt over her head, she looked up and caught Marsh watching her. She smiled tentatively and stepped up onto a toehold on the rear of the truck.

Marsh's face held a look that she couldn't quite decipher as he held out his hand, which she took. He hauled her easily up and over the tailgate, and Willy chose a likely spot to sit near the back of the truck bed, returning Dusti and Jack's cheery greeting as she did so.

At that moment, Marsh had flashed back six years to when he'd last seen her during a Christmastime visit to Eden.

Chapter Nine

Willy had gone caroling with the Youth Fellowship and was in the Grays' kitchen helping Marsh's mother prepare hot chocolate for the chilly carolers when Marsh arrived home from college for the holiday break.

She stood absolutely still for a few moments when he came through the door from the backporch. He thought she'd never looked more appealing than she had in her slacks, snow boots, and college sweatshirt. Her cheeks were still rosy from the cold December air, and a few melting snowflakes in her hair caught the light from the overhead fixture.

It was like a blow to his solar plexus when she said a brief, rather impersonal "hello." Then she turned back to setting mugs of hot chocolate onto a tray which she quickly carried into the living room to the waiting carolers....

* * *

As Marsh gave a hand up to Vi Dunaway and several of the other hayriders, he admonished himself not to think about those times. Since they had talked the other night and danced together last night, much of the strain had eased away. They could be friends again. *Maybe not quite like the old days. But then, did he really want it to be like the old days?*

Phil joined his wife in a spot just behind the truck cab, and asked in general, "Are we all here? Anyone expecting someone else?"

"I think Greg Anfinson's coming," said one of the boys sitting across from Willy.

"Okay, we'll give him a few more minutes," Phil replied good-naturedly, as he spread a blanket across his and Vi's laps.

"This may be him," said Marsh, as a pickup truck slowed to turn into the church lot. He returned the wave of a middle-aged lady in the driver's seat as a sandy-haired boy of about thirteen jumped out and ran toward the farm truck.

Greg scrambled over the tailgate. "Sorry I'm late," he said as he spotted his friend and settled into a place in the the thick hay beside him.

"Glad you made it, Greg," replied Phil. "I think we're ready to go now. Keep your heads down, everyone." He tapped on the window behind him. "All set, Jonas."

In the meantime, Marsh sat down beside Willy and pulled his cap more securely onto his head. He turned to her once the truck had left the parking lot and started west down the county road.

Reaching behind her, he lifted the hood on her sweatshirt. "Here, Willy, you'd better put your hood up. Don't want you to get an earache." He fitted it over her head.

She looked up at him wonderingly as she tied the strings under her chin. "How on earth did you remember that the wind could give me an earache?"

"Oh, there's very little that I've forgotten, Willy." His grin and the sparkle in his eyes made her wonder just what he was remembering.

She groaned internally and tensed as he left his arm around her, snuggling her near him as he scrunched down to get his head out of the wind.

"Relax, little sis. My shoulder's softer than the side of the truck. After all, it isn't the first time we've sat together on a hayride," he added in an undertone.

She turned her head toward him and spoke quietly in what could only be described as a hiss. "Yes, but we were kids then. We're adults now and helping the Dunaways chaperone. What'll everyone think?"

"Well, if they think anything it'll probably be that we're friends and are enjoying the hayride. Okay?" His raised left eyebrow and the set of his jaw told her that he thought she was being foolish.

She breathed out a little snort of air. "Okay, you're probably right. It's just that I'm not used to being around you again."

"I hope you'll get used to it," he replied in a low tone.

She looked back at him in an attempt to read his face, but he had turned to speak to the boy and girl on the other side of him. When Vi started the kids singing, Willy joined in with Marsh soon following.

An hour later, Willy stood in the women's changing room at Bradford Lake and tugged her new swimsuit down over her backside and up over her chest. "Arrgh," she muttered as the suit slipped back down displaying more cleavage than Willy would have liked.

"You look great in your new swimsuit, Willy," said Vi Dunaway with a smile. "Very trim and stylish."

"Thanks, Vi. Can you believe I shopped for three hours this afternoon, and this still isn't quite what I was looking for—it shows a bit too much of me."

"Oh, don't worry. The girls are mostly in bikinis, so our one-piece suits look mature and proper in comparison." The lady laughed and adjusted the straps on her own dark green suit with a chartreuse diagonal stripe across the front.

Willy smiled in gratitude. "You look very nice too, Vi. That style suits you."

"Thank you, dear. What you really mean is that it's *slimming*," Vi said with a grin as she smoothed the suit over her ample hips.

Willy returned her smile as they turned in their baskets to the attendant to hold their clothing while they swam. Willy thought that Vi was a really nice lady whom she was glad to get to know. They stepped out onto the walkway before the changing rooms.

At the end of it, near the beach area, Phil and Marsh stood talking with a group of the teenagers already in their swimsuits. At a word from Phil, Marsh suddenly turned and looked toward them.

Willy sucked in a sharp breath and gritted her teeth at the sight of him. *Oh, my, how could she ignore him when he looked so handsome?*

She saw his hands clutch the ends of the white towel draped around his neck a little tighter, and she was afraid to make eye contact.

Knowing her face was flushed, she draped her pink towel around her shoulders, pulled it together over her cleavage, lifted her chin, and decided she would not let her awareness of Marsh interfere with her enjoyment of the evening.

As they neared the group, Vi said, "Thanks for waiting for us slowpokes, gang."

"Our pleasure," answered her husband. "Say, are you two lovely ladies going our way?" He slipped Vi's hand into his and they walked toward the sand and water.

Willy envied their obvious deep attachment to each other, and let out a breath she hadn't been aware she was holding.

She followed the group and started a little when Marsh fell into step beside her.

"Nice suit," he commented nonchalantly. "May I whistle?"

"No!" She shot him a sideways look that would have killed a lesser man. "It's new. I didn't bring one with me from Katy and had to shop for one today. The only one still at home was the . . ." She hesitated, knowing that in her nervousness she was saying too much. "A bikini."

Marsh raised a quizzical eyebrow. "Hmmm."

"Don't start," Willy said snappishly.

Marsh just grinned and began humming a tune that sounded suspiciously like an ode to a yellow polka dot bikini.

"Stop that, Marsh!" she exclaimed as she elbowed him in the ribs. The small smile that lifted the corners of her mouth belied her sharp tone of voice.

Marsh laughed but grabbed his ribs in an exaggerated display of pain. "Ow! You've jabbed me in the same place so often over the years that there's this little spot that twinges when it sees your elbow come near it."

"Oh, pooh! Sure, it does," she retorted. "I guess you'll just have to keep your distance, won't you?"

Marsh had paused at the foot of the ladder up to the diving boards to lay his towel over a rail. Turning to her, he spoke quietly but firmly. "Easier said than done, Willy."

Willy caught her breath at his words. Then he turned and climbed up the ladder. She hesitated only briefly before hanging her towel beside his and following him. Reminding herself that she was here to chaperone and have fun with the kids, she waited at the back of the platform while Marsh dived. Giving him time to clear the diving area, she walked to the end of the board, bounced, and executed an almost perfect jack-knife into the water.

Later, after time spent diving, Willy enjoyed a swim out to the anchored raft with Dusti and several of the other girls. Then the whole group played a rowdy game of watertag. She was dunked several times. All in all, she had a great time.

Phil and Marsh dried off and dressed early in order to build the campfire which was to the perfect point for roasting wieners by the time everyone else had changed and joined them in the picnic grove.

Everything tasted delicious. Willy found she ate two hot dogs with no trouble at all and still had plenty of room for potato chips and lots of sweet toasted marshmallows. Marsh appeared at her side with a peeled green stick on which four charred marshmallows hung.

"O-ooo, perfect!" she exclaimed. "Just the way I

love them." She pulled a couple off the stick, popped them into her mouth, and licked her sticky fingers.

"Yep, I remember," he said around the remainder of the burned globs. "You know, I'm glad I told the Dunaway kids I'd come along. It's still a lot of fun, isn't it?"

She smiled at him in the darkness relieved only by the glow from the campfire and the security lights back near the parking area. Happy that he looked so relaxed and carefree, she agreed. "Yes, it always was fun, and it still is. I'd bet it always will be."

For just a moment, they looked directly into each other's eyes and something passed unspoken between them. Marsh nodded his head before looking back at the fire.

Willy swallowed the lump that had formed in her throat. "Things will be all right, Marsh," she whispered. "It just takes time."

Later, when the campfire was out and the area cleaned up, the group climbed back into the farm truck for the ride home to Eden.

Willy sat in the same spot as before. She adjusted and tied her hood, then shook out her blanket. Pulling her knees up, she tucked the blanket around her until she resembled a cocoon. Marsh sat beside her and did the same.

Once the truck was on the road, the air being cooler than earlier in the evening, Willy burrowed deeper into her blanket, trying not to shiver.

"Cold, Willy?" Marsh asked, noticing her shivers.

"Uh-huh," she murmured.

He lifted his blanket and spread it across the two of them. In the process, he put his left arm around her and snuggled her closer.

Willy felt a moment of panic, not knowing if she wanted to sit so near him again. But the warmth of two blankets, not to mention Marsh's warm chest, chased her chill away.

"That's better, isn't it?" he said and scooted down a bit until his chin was resting on the top of her head.

Willy sat quietly, wondering what he was thinking. She smiled and stifled a giggle that welled up in her throat. The closeness didn't appear to be a problem at all for Marsh. He had just fallen asleep.

Relaxing against him, she closed her eyes and very much enjoyed the rest of the hayride.

Willy awoke and stretched when her bedside alarm went off on Sunday morning. She'd had a sound night's sleep undisturbed by any dreams of Marshall Gray, but he was immediately in her thoughts upon awakening.

Willy smiled as she remembered how Marsh started awake when the farm truck came to a halt in the church lot the previous night. Confused, he pushed back the blankets, looked at her, and mumbled sleepily, "Willy?"

"We're back at the church, Marsh," she answered.

"Oh, right," he agreed, sounding a bit more awake.

They gathered their things together and climbed down out of the truck. Shaking out their blankets and brushing bits of hay off their clothing, they waited with the Dunaways until they were sure that all the teenagers had a ride home.

On the short drive to her house, Marsh rolled down his window to let the cool air blow into his face.

"Are you sure you'll make it home okay, Marsh?" she asked when he stopped in her driveway.

"Uh-huh, I'm better now. Sorry I conked out on you, Willy. I must've been more tired than I realized." He gave her a crooked grin.

"That's all right. You've been working hard lately, and you've been upset too, so your body just relaxed tonight and let you sleep." She warmly returned his smile.

"I wasn't actually asleep the whole time, Willy," he said as he reached across and tucked a stray curl back from her cheek. He rested his hand on the back of her head.

She quickly turned to look at him. The intensity of his gaze hit her almost like a physical blow.

A soft "ohh" escaped her lips and she felt just the slightest pressure from his hand as he started to urge her toward him.

She wanted to go, but instead said, "Don't," in a strangled little voice, "not—not now."

He pulled his hand back and rested both of them on the steering wheel. After a moment, he said, "You're right, Willy. It's too soon to kiss you." He closed his eyes. "It doesn't stop my thoughts or my feelings though. I only hope that we can spend more time together, now that I've found you again."

He opened his eyes and looked at her as he said those last words, and she thought her heart would burst with the emotion she felt flowing from him.

She pulled in a deep breath. "I—I want to spend time with you too, Marsh. It's just that we have to be . . ." She paused, looking for the best word to express how she felt. "We have to be cautious, and we weren't tonight."

Marsh replied, "Cautious? All right, I'll agree with that. So, you're saying we should just stay with our old friendship. Big brother Marsh and little sister Willy? I could do that, if it's what you want—for awhile."

"Yes, we can do that for awhile. We need to get to know each other again. Then we can see where we want to go from there." Willy bit her lower lip. She knew where she wanted it to go, but she wanted Marshall to be sure also. She didn't want him on the rebound from a disastrous marriage.

"Don't look so worried, little sis. We can handle it. Let's start by getting you into the house and me home." Marsh grabbed her blanket and opened the truck door.

On the porch, Willy unlocked the door. "Goodnight. Will I see you in church tomorrow, Marsh?"

"Sure. Let's plan to spend some time together after church too. We'll have some lunch and go see your mother. Things old friends can do." He grinned at her, sending a little shiver all the way to her toes.

"Okay," she responded with a grin of her own. "Night, bro!" She slipped inside and left him standing on the front porch . . .

Willy smiled, hopped out of bed with a bounce, and stretched luxuriously. She felt good, and she knew it was because she was going to spend the day with Marsh.

After she and the cats had eaten their breakfasts, she ran back upstairs for a shower and shampoo. In her bedroom, she decided to go casual in a simple pink scoopneck cotton pullover shirt tucked into the waist of an A-line skirt in a deep rose hue. It looked to be a hot day, so this time she left the pantyhose in a drawer when she slipped on her brown sandals. After fixing her face, she turned before the mirror on the back of the hall closet door.

She looked cool, comfortable, and very happy. She grinned and reminded herself not to look *too* happy, especially when she looked at Marsh, or people would suspect how she really felt about him. She practiced a look of friendly, sisterly admiration, and failed miserably. Laughing, she went downstairs, out to the garage, and drove her mother's car to church.

As on the previous Sunday, she joined Uncle Karl and Aunt Hilda in their pew. She wondered if Marsh would slip in late again and sit beside her. As she looked over the bulletin, she somehow believed that he would. Her positive thoughts paid off a few minutes later when, right before the opening hymn, he sat down.

Flashing a smile her way, he said, "Good morning, Willy, may I sit here with you?" He took in the lovely sight she made as she smiled back.

"Good morning, Marsh. Of course." He looked handsome and very comfortable in tan slacks and a tan and white striped cotton dress shirt that opened at the throat. She felt a little giddy.

"How are you today?" he asked politely.

"Very good, thank you. And you?" she replied demurely.

"Just fine. It's going to be a lovely day."

Willy smiled in anticipation of what that might mean.

The music began for the choir's processional and they stood to share a hymnal. This time she wasn't nervous as they each held a side of the songbook and joined in the singing.

Later in the worship service, when the pastor had

begun his sermon, she noticed that Marsh laid his left hand on the wooden pew between them. When he waggled his fingers at her, she glanced at him. He looked straight ahead, seemingly absorbed in the message. She casually laid her right hand on the pew beside his, and he covered it with his, giving it a warm squeeze. They sat in that position through the rest of the sermon. Willy believed she had never felt happier.

When the service ended, they filed out into the sunshine. Marsh talked with Karl for a few minutes, then his parents, Frank and Eva Gray, joined them.

"Hello, Willy. So nice to see you again." Eva, a petite brunette in her early fifties with Marsh's greenish hazel eyes, greeted Willy with a warm hug. Eva had long been one of Willy's favorite people.

Her husband, Frank, a quiet man, tall and slender in the manner of Marsh, hugged her next. "You're as pretty as a picture, girl. We'd heard you were here for the summer."

"How's your mother getting along, dear?" asked Eva.

"Much better, thank you. She had a difficult week, caught a virus, but was doing well when I saw her yesterday morning."

Marsh's father asked him where he had been keeping himself. "It seems we have to come to church to see you," he added with a chuckle and was joined in laughter by the others.

"Well, Dad, I guess church is better than a lot of places where you could run into me," Marsh replied dryly. Then he added, "I've just been busy working. Oh, can't forget Friday night's dance. Had to kick up my heels a little there. Last evening, Willy and I found we had both volunteered to help chaperone the YF hayride which turned out to be fun."

Willy added, "Yes, it was a lot of fun. Vi and Phil Dunaway do a great job with the youth group."

Frank asked Karl how the fund for the second watertank truck was doing, and after a few more minutes of conversation, the group broke up.

Both older couples had asked Marsh and Willy if they would like to come home with them for Sunday dinner. Marsh declined for the two of them politely. He said that he and Willy had made plans to have a bite of lunch together and then visit Grace.

Walking toward their vehicles at the far side of the church lot, Marsh spoke, sounding a bit proud of himself. "There, little sis, I think I handled that well enough. Our families know we've seen each other casually and will most likely continue."

Willy grinned in return at Marsh's pleased look. "Uh-huh. You set the right tone. Casual friends doing casual things together, like old friends do."

"Right." He paused by her car as she got into the driver's seat. "I'll be by your house in a few minutes, and don't change a thing. Dad was right, you look as pretty as a picture in that outfit."

She glanced at him through her open window. Feeling flattered by his compliment, she nevertheless answered back saucily. "Just a chip off the old block, huh, big brother? By the way, where are we going for lunch?"

"I'll surprise you. Now get home, little sis, so I can pick you up. Time's a-wastin'!"

She started the car and put it into gear. "Bye, Marsh." Her lovely laugh followed him to his truck.

* * *

Expecting Marsh to drive out of town to either Piqua or Harris Mills, Willy was surprised when he pulled the pickup into the parking lot behind "Kate's Place" on Main Street. Kate's was a popular dining out spot for the locals who enjoyed her home cooking and could depend on the quality and generous quantities of the daily specials. Kate's also did a good business with the truckers who came through Eden on the state highway.

Marsh and Willy had both often frequented Kate's as teenagers as she kept a well-stocked soda fountain and welcomed the local kids as customers.

"Gosh, it's been ages since I've been to Kate's. I wonder if it's changed any? But are you sure we should stop here, Marsh? Everyone is going to know us." She looked at him, a tiny frown on her forehead as he switched off the engine.

Marsh turned to her and smiled. "That's the idea. We go where people know us, and they get used to seeing us together right out in the open, having a pleasant, friendly lunch." He emphasized the word *friendly,* and Willy had to laugh.

"Marsh, you are a very devious man. Why hadn't I ever noticed that before?"

He raised an eyebrow at her. "Devious, huh? I guess you were too busy noticing all my other *good* qualities—honesty, loyalty, trustworthiness . . ."

"Okay, okay," she interrupted, "you were a good boy scout! Let's go eat."

They walked up a sidewalk beside a flowerbed filled with red and white petunias that ran along the side of the building. Under a red awning, Marsh opened the outer door and Willy preceded him into the restaurant.

Heads turned curiously to see who had just entered,

and Willy and Marsh smiled and nodded to several neighbors whom they had known for years.

Kate's was a casual place, so they found an empty booth themselves beside a window that looked out on the street.

Willy smiled warmly across the table at Marsh. "It's changed, but it's still much the same too, isn't it? It still *feels* the same anyway."

"Yes, still welcoming and comfortable. Kate has spruced the place up a bit since our high school days though."

"Remember the old gray formica tabletops?" Willy asked as she ran a hand over the smooth surface of the unmarred white table. "And the old maroon seats? These red seat coverings are a nice improvement." Her eyes sparkled as she took in the red and white window curtains, the white tiled floor and the red carnations on each table.

Marsh enjoyed watching her expressive face as she looked around the restaurant. "The food's still good too," he said. "I've stopped in for supper several times in the last few months. The last time I had the Wednesday special—a great pot roast."

"What days do you have to go before you've tried all the specials, Marsh?" Willy asked teasingly.

He chuckled and began counting them off on his left hand. "Let's see, I think Tuesday, Saturday, and today, Sunday." He paused to smile at the pretty young waitress who placed a glass of ice water before each of them. "Hello, Jess."

"Hi, Marsh," the girl said with a shy smile.

"Willy, I don't know if you remember Jessica Miller, Kate's granddaughter. Jess, Willy Heidler."

"Hello, Willy. I thought I recognized you."

"It's been a long time, hasn't it. I'm happy to see you again, Jessica. Tell Kate hello for me when you see her." Willy thought the quiet, pretty little girl she remembered had grown into a lovely young woman.

"I will. She's in the kitchen today. She always does all the cooking herself on Sundays. What can I get for you?" she added, her pencil ready to take down the orders.

"What's today's special?" Willy asked with a mischievous glance at Marsh.

"Chicken pot pie, one of Grandma's best."

"Great, that's what I'll have," Marsh said with no trace of hesitation. "Shall we make that two, Willy?"

"Yes, it sounds very good."

"Okay," Jessica said as she jotted it down on her pad. "That comes with green beans and applesauce on the side. What would you like to drink?"

"Coffee." He looked questioningly at Willy, who nodded. "Two coffees, then."

"I'll be back shortly." The waitress smiled and left them.

After Jessica had served the coffee and a small basket of homemade rolls, Marsh sat stirring non-dairy creamer into his cup. His expression was pensive.

Willy asked, "You look lost in thought, Marsh." She took a sip of her black coffee.

"I was just wondering when you'll know if the teaching position is yours."

"Possibly as early as tomorrow. Mr. Dunbar did say in a week. I'm excited at the opportunity. I like Katy and the school there, but Eden has truly always felt like home." She smiled across the table at him.

"So, you'd be happy to come back home, live in Eden again?" he asked soberly.

"Yes, I think I would—for several reasons," she replied as she glanced out the window at a tractor-trailer that rolled through on Main Street. Then she looked back at Marsh.

His next question surprised her, as did the intensity with which he asked it. His hands folded around his cup, he looked her in the eye, and said, "Are you seeing anyone in Texas that you're serious about, Willy?"

She looked away briefly as she felt a rush of warmth to her face. "Well, no. No one that I'm seriously interested in." She glanced back at him and caught an expression of relief on his handsome face.

His serious look gave way to a smile. "I'm glad, Willy, but I'm surprised too. What's wrong with those Texas men that one of them hasn't put a ring on your hand yet?"

She took another swallow of coffee and looked at him over the rim. "A couple have tried, but I wasn't— they weren't . . ." She was saved by Jessica arriving with their lunch. "My goodness, that looks wonderful," she said, and as they began to eat she hoped Marsh wouldn't ask anything else about her Texas men friends.

They declined Jessica's offer of dessert, and left Kate's Place to drive to the farm. Marsh seemed anxious to show it to her, and he kept up a running monologue as he drove.

"I'd always liked the Brown farm. I think I was really fortunate to come along just as it was being put on the market. It was in remarkably good shape for an older house too. The Browns had done a little remodeling over the years, and I'm in the process of doing a bit more. But in general, such as the roof, plumbing, wiring, and the furnace, I lucked out."

Willy listened attentively with a little smile on her face. She enjoyed hearing the enthusiasm in his voice.

As they turned up the lane, he stopped talking and reached over to give her left hand a gentle squeeze. Willy suddenly felt very excited and leaned forward in her seat to catch a first glimpse of the house.

"Oh, Marsh, you're right. It really is still a lovely house. I can only remember being inside a couple of times, but I've always remembered those bay windows, and I love a big front porch."

He parked the truck near the front walk, and they got out. Marsh came around and took her hand in his as Willy looked around, then walked with him to the porch.

"The outside will need paint in another year or so," Marsh stated, "but right now I'm more concerned with renovating the inside."

He dropped her hand to unlock the door, then stepped back to let her precede him into the front hall.

Willy gasped in surprise. "I don't remember this beautiful flooring," she said as she looked at an expanse of oakboards before her. Then her eyes found the intricately carved newel post at the base of the graceful handrail on the stairway, also oak.

"It was covered with well-worn maroon carpet. I was as surprised as you to find this oak flooring beneath it," Marsh informed her as he led her under an arch into the living room.

"And you did the same in here?" she asked, noting the bare oak floor.

"Yes," Marsh replied. He smiled as she hurried to the wide bay window that looked out over the small front yard and toward the woods.

"Such a pretty view," she murmured as she ran a

hand over the wooden windowseat. It would be a cozy spot to sit, with a few bright padded cushions and pillows added. Willy turned and said, "I *thought* it had a fireplace," as she joined Marsh before it.

"Look at this mantel, Willy, solid cherrywood. One of the first things I did when I moved in was polish it." He grinned down at her as he leaned his right elbow on the mantelpiece.

Willy laughed. "You look like the lord of the manor, Marsh. All you need is a pipe, a brocade jacket, and a proper British accent."

"I say, m'dear," he tried an imitation—something near Prince Charles with a tinge of John Cleese—and laughed. "I don't smoke, and I'm more of a terry cloth robe man, actually, but it does feel good to have my own home."

"I hope you'll be very happy here, Marsh," Willy said with sincerity. "You deserve some happiness."

Marsh looked at her for a long moment, a myriad of emotions passing across his face, his throat working before he suddenly reached forward and pulled her into his arms. Pressing her face against his shoulder, he buried his face in her fluffy curls.

Briefly startled by the sudden move, Willy nevertheless hugged him in return, patting Marsh's back when he said, "Thank you, Willy. I hope you'll be happy too, and I hope you're able to move back to Eden. That alone would make me very happy."

He lifted his head and smoothed her curls with both his hands as he smiled down at her.

She looked at him, her expression serious. "You'd like me to come back to Eden, Marsh?"

"More than anything! More than anything," he repeated. "I finally feel that things are coming together for me. I've been living in a sort of limbo for the past six months. Now I want to start to live again. I hope you'll be here too, Willy. That would mean a lot to me."

His words filled her with such elation, she had to hold back the urge to throw her arms around his neck. Instead, she took a deep breath and clasped her hands before her to keep them from touching him. "Marsh," she said, "I really hope that I *can* be here too."

It was the closest they had come to expressing feelings for one another, and the enormity of it seemed to hold them spellbound for a few minutes. Each gazed into the other's eyes; then Marsh rested his hands on her shoulders.

"Do you know how very much I want to kiss you right now, this very minute?" he said, a husky edge to his quiet voice.

Willy let out a little sigh. "Yes, I do, because I want it too," she whispered.

He gathered her close and nuzzled the top of her head before he said, "But we won't. We decided last night that we'd just be friends for awhile. But my dear sweet girl, one of these days I'm going to come courting, and you won't know what hit you!" He released her, settling her a little away from him, and chuckled.

Willy giggled in response to his words. "Courting? Marsh, that's such an old-fashioned word, but I love the idea. Sounds like it could be fun."

"You better believe it!" Marsh placed his hands on her waist, lifted her, and swung a laughing Willy around the empty living room before putting her back onto her feet. "Now, my girl, let me show you the rest of the house."

"There's a formal dining room through these double

doors," he told her as he demonstrated how the pocket doors slid into the wall. Then they walked through a single swinging door that led into the kitchen.

"My goodness, you've done a lot of work in here. This is so bright and cheerful!" Willy exclaimed as she turned and looked in all directions.

Marsh leaned against a counter. "The major changes so far have been in here, plus I added a bath upstairs. Of course, I had help with the plumbing as that's not my thing, but I've always thought a kitchen is the heart of a home, and I wanted to get it up and running. The other rooms and getting some furniture can come more slowly." He smiled at her pleased expression as she wandered around the room.

Marsh had retained the older cupboards, designed with small panes of glass in the upper doors, but freshened them with a coat of pale cream paint nicely complementing the new forest green countertops. There was a stainless steel double sink under the window. An electric range, a large side-by-side refrigerator-freezer, and a dishwasher in white had been fitted into their places. Under it all was new linoleum in a light cream with a gold pattern.

Willy complimented Marsh on his work, commenting that she especially liked the island work area he had added. "I'm glad the back bay window is still here. You came up with some nice ideas, Marsh. The colors are great too."

"Well, I had some help. I pored over kitchen and bath do-it-yourself magazines before I settled on this layout." He led her to an alcove to the left of the backdoor. "Here's the laundry room." He patted a washer and dryer that matched the kitchen appliances. "Some nice pantry shelves along this wall for extra storage. Through this door is the original bath. It was in good condition, though it's the one I painted yesterday."

Willy noted the new pale gold paint before he took her through a narrow second door leading into what Marsh pointed out as a downstairs bedroom. "Or it could be used in another way, but for now I've been sleeping here."

Willy glimpsed his air mattress and sleeping bag in a corner before she followed him out of the room and back into the kitchen. He turned down the hall that led back to the front of the house.

"This will be my den or home office," he said as he opened a door across from the living room. "My parents gave me this desk. It had been in Mother's family for several generations."

Willy ran a hand lovingly over the smooth surface of the antique mahogany desk. "It's truly beautiful, Marsh."

"The only thing from the Cincinnati apartment I wanted to keep," he said a bit tersely. "That, and my books and stereo," he added in a lighter tone. "Come on, let's take a quick tour of the upstairs before we drive into Piqua." He took her hand and tugged her toward the stairway.

As they peeked into the bedrooms, Willy said, "This house is larger than I knew. How many bedrooms?"

"Only five." Marsh laughed. "I have hopes of filling them up one day. I still want to have a family. Do you still want children someday, Willy?" He raised a dark eyebrow quizzically as he opened another door.

Though he spoke nonchalantly, Willy sensed that her answer was very important to Marsh. "Yes, I do, very much," she answered quietly. "In fact, I've been thinking about babies and marriage a lot lately."

Marsh paused and looked back at her, a slow smile growing on his handsome face. Willy felt a blush moving up her throat. "I mean . . ." she tried to qualify her statement, but he interrupted.

"I know what you mean—I understand perfectly." Marsh's mellow voice took on a vibrant quality. Then he turned abruptly to show her into the master bedroom and the new bath he had added.

It could be reached from that room as well as the hall, but he had also cut an additional door into a back bedroom. "In order to fit in a bath up here, I had to make this back room much smaller. Then as an afterthought I had this door cut into it. The room seemed perfect for a nursery. With the connecting doors, a baby could be heard easily at night. The room would be fine for a playroom later, or perhaps a sewing room. Lots of possibilities."

Willy laughed, "Yes, but if you're planning to fill these bedrooms, it'll be busy as a nursery for many years to come!"

"I hope so," he replied with a broad grin. Then, a bit more seriously, "Do you like the house, Willy?"

"I love it, Marsh. You're making it into a lovely home."

As they started back down the stairs, he asked, "How would you decorate it? I like your taste in color and style, always have. What do you think would look good?"

Willy, pleased that he'd consult her opinion, replied, "Well, I must admit as you've shown me around, I've been mentally choosing colors and placing furniture. A habit of mine when I'm in a new place," she added as an excuse. "I like the shade of cream paint in the kitchen. I'd use that through all the other rooms as it's a warm but neutral tone. Then you could add color in various ways—upholstery, curtains, carpets—as much or as little as you wanted."

She paused as Marsh locked the door behind them. They had gotten into the truck before Marsh said, "Go on, Willy, I'm listening."

"Some areas accented with wallpaper add character too," she continued. "I like wallpaper myself. As for carpeting, the oak floors are so pretty, it'd be a shame to cover them completely. Perhaps a runner down the hall and some area rugs in the dining and living rooms?" she added, glancing at Marsh's profile to gauge his reaction to her suggestions.

He flashed a quick smile her way. "Sounds good. Gives me a lot to think about. I'll re-carpet the den and probably the downstairs bedroom though. I checked the flooring and, for some reason, it's not hardwood and hasn't held up as well. We'll have to give your Uncle Karl a visit and stock up on that shade of cream paint. How are you at handling a paint roller, Willy?"

"Passable," she drawled. "Looking for some free labor, are you?"

"Let's just say, it would give you a vested interest in the house and us a reason to spend time together. Besides, I think you'd look cute with paint on your nose," he teased.

Chapter Ten

Willy spent Monday morning cleaning the house and doing laundry. She paid special attention to her mother's small downstairs bedroom as she hoped she would be released from the hospital within a few days.

It looked good when she and Marsh visited Grace on Sunday afternoon. Grace was practicing walking with crutches as a prerequisite to going home.

Grace was delighted to see Marsh again, and the three of them had a pleasant visit remembering some fun and special times from years ago. Willy told her that the hayride had been well attended and a lot of fun.

When Grace asked about Marsh's new house, he had very proudly described the renovations completed so far. Willy added her own remarks about how nice everything looked and the efficiency of the kitchen area. Marsh told Grace of Willy's decorating ideas that he'd solicited, ending with the fact that he had coerced her into helping paint.

Willy sat down at the kitchen table with a tall glass of iced tea and thought of the previous day's events.

She and Marsh were about to say good-bye to her mother when Bill came in making late afternoon rounds. His face lit up in pleased surprise at seeing them there together.

"Hello," he said, "it's great to see you both again." Bill gave Willy's hand a squeeze as she returned his greeting, then shook Marsh's heartily.

"How's it going, Bill?" Marsh asked.

Bill smiled. "Very well, thanks. And thanks too, Marsh, for introducing me to Marie. She's agreed to have dinner with me tonight."

"That's great, Bill," Marsh and Willy answered nearly together. Willy added rather teasingly, "I know from experience that the Bellingham for dinner makes a good first impression."

Bill laughed and Marsh looked puzzled. Willy explained, "Bill and I went to dinner there a week or so ago. It's a lovely restaurant near Harris Mills."

"As a matter of fact, that *is* where we're going tonight," Bill said. Then, turning to Grace's bedside, "If you'll excuse me, I'll do my job here so I can complete my rounds early tonight. Hope to see you both again soon."

"We were about to leave," Marsh said. "Goodnight, Mrs. Heidler. I enjoyed talking with you again."

"I enjoyed it too, dear. Goodnight, Willy," Grace said, kissing her daughter's cheek as Willy leaned down. "Have a nice evening."

Willy hugged her mother. "Thanks, Mom. I'll be down tomorrow."

"See you, Bill," said Marsh as he and Willy turned to go.

"Give our best to Marie," Willy added with a little wave of her hand.

Bill smiled as he nodded in reply, his hands busy with Grace's bandages.

The phone ringing brought Willy's thoughts back to the present and she hurried to answer it, thinking it could be the hospital or possibly Sarah, or even Marsh. Thinking of Marsh brought a smile to her face. The last twenty-four hours had certainly eased the tension even hearing his name had once caused her. She hoped Bill was right when he said that he thought Marsh loved her.

"Hello," she said and mentally crossed her fingers when she heard Ted Dunbar identify himself.

He was calling to inform her that the school board had voted to offer her a one-year contract. Willy was delighted and told him so. The salary he mentioned was less than her Katy wages, but she accepted and made arrangements to go into his office on Tuesday morning to sign a contract.

"Thank you very much, Mr. Dunbar," she added, "I'll be so happy to be living in Eden again."

As she replaced the receiver, she thought, *You have no idea how very happy I am, Mr. Dunbar!*

Willy ran upstairs to get her purse, looked through it for her address book, and returned to the phone. Sitting down on the bench, she took a deep breath and composed what she would say to her school superintendent in Katy.

Quickly dialing the office number, she was put through to Mrs. DeSoto. Upon hearing Willy's candid explanation of her mother's ill health and of her opportunity to teach in her hometown and be near family and old friends again, the superintendent was understanding. She assured Willy that there'd be no problem letting her out of the second year of her current contract. She appreciated her prompt notification and wished her well in the future.

In turn, Willy expressed her appreciation, thanked Mrs. DeSoto, and assured her she would send a formal letter of resignation in the next day's mail.

Hanging up the phone, Willy leaped to her feet, pumped her fist in the air, and yelled, "Yes!" Cleo, who had been asleep on a cushion in the corner of the hall, stretched lazily, shot Willy a look that seemed to say, "You're disturbing my beauty rest, girl!" and snuggled herself back into a cozy ball of fur.

Excited by her good fortune, Willy made herself sit back down. Her mind raced as she decided who to call. *Marsh? Mom? Betsy?* She realized Betsy would be at work now so it would be necessary to phone her in the evening. They would have to make plans to move Willy's things back to Ohio. Luckily, she didn't have much in the way of furniture, but there were books, some kitchen things, the rest of her clothes, and such. *Oh, my car's there, too!* Willy laughed aloud at herself for nearly forgetting her little green car. She knew she'd miss Betsy, a good friend and a super roommate, but she also knew Betsy would be pleased by Willy's plans.

Forty-five minutes later, Willy had talked with her mother, left a message with Paige for Mary, spoken with Aunt Hilda, and chatted with Sarah. All were delighted to hear the news.

Grace had news of her own as Old Doc had set Wednesday as a release date, providing she felt comfortable on the crutches and there were no signs of re-infection. Willy was ecstatic to hear that.

"Everything's looking up, Mom!" she exclaimed.

"It certainly is, dear. Since you have plans to make and an important letter to write, please don't feel you have to come down today. I'm fine, and I'm in the middle of a romantic paperback. The heroine is about to come face to face with the man of her dreams," she added with a satisfied laugh.

Joining her mother in laughter, Willy replied, "Hurrah for her! Okay, Mom, I'll talk to you later then. Bye."

Willy had just picked up the phonebook to locate the number of Bertram Jones' law office when the phone rang, causing her to jump. A trace of laughter still lingering in her voice, she answered.

"Hi, Willy," Marsh said. "What's up? I've been trying to get through to you for ages. I've got good news, sweetheart!"

"Me, too, Marsh." *Sweetheart?* She paused as the word and the possible significance of his using it sank into her brain. "Oh, what's happened?" Willy felt a tremor of excitement shoot through her body. She held her breath in anticipation of his next words.

"I completed my probationary period with Bert a few days ago. This morning, he called me into his office and offered me a full partnership. I very gladly accepted."

Willy expelled her breath. "I'm so happy for you, Marsh! That's wonderful news."

"Thank you, I'm truly pleased. This is the kind of law I've always hoped to practice one day, so it's full speed ahead and no looking back," he said before pausing, his voice deepening with emotion. "Willy, I hope you'll be with me, side by side, together for the rest of our lives."

"Marsh," she whispered, "do you know what you just said? Was that a—a proposal?" Her voice squeaked a little, and Marsh chuckled.

"Sure was, sweetheart! A marriage proposal. You don't have to answer now. Consider it, and in the meantime, I'll start that courtship I promised you. Where would you like to go for dinner tonight? We should celebrate." He paused and waited for a reply.

Willy giggled and cried at the same time. "Marsh, you silly goose, asking me something as important as that over the phone! But, I promise I'll consider it." *Boy, will I ever!* She brushed the tears away with the back of her hand and sniffled.

"Willy, are you crying? Are you okay? I'm sorry; I should have waited to ask you, but, well..." His voice trailed off.

"Marsh, honey, I'm fine. I'm very happy for you and for me too. Oh, I nearly forgot my news! I got the teaching position here. I sign the contract tomorrow. So, we have two reasons to celebrate tonight."

"Great! Congratulations, Willy. I knew they'd hire you. You'll be back in Eden as we both wanted. It'll be much easier to court you than if you were still in Texas," he added with a chuckle.

"Definitely!" she said with enthusiasm, returning his laugh. "Oh, let's go up to Lorenzo's Landing on the lake for a chicken dinner. It's been ages since I've been there."

"Fine, Willy. Good food, dancing to the jukebox, a moonlight stroll out onto the pier, and a romantic drive along the lakeshore—all wonderful courting scenarios. Say, I'm really getting into this courtship thing, aren't I?"

"Uh-huh, sounds absolutely grand to me. I'll be

looking forward to it. I'll be ready about six or so? Okay?"

"That should work as I have a couple of stops to make before I head home. See you, love."

"Bye." She hugged the phone receiver as she savored his words. He'd called her sweetheart and his love. *He wants me to marry him!* Willy practically floated into her father's den where she forced herself to sit down at his old typewriter and compose an intelligent, business-like letter of resignation to the Katy school superintendent. She did so, but a little smile never left her face.

When Willy answered the door in response to Marsh's gentle rap, she gasped in surprise and delight when he withdrew a bouquet of a dozen red roses from behind his back.

"Oh, how beautiful they are!" she exclaimed as he handed them to her.

"Not nearly as beautiful as you, Willy," he said with a smile, admiring the way she looked in a knee-length dress that had tiny blue flowers scattered over a silky white material. It swished enticingly as she walked toward him.

"Oh, now *that* was smooth. You look pretty handsome yourself." He wore a monochromatic gray business suit, dress shirt, and tie. She returned his smile and lifted the roses to smell the lovely fragrance. Her dark eyes dancing, she tiptoed to kiss him on the cheek. "Thank you, Marsh. Was this one of the stops you had to make?"

"Uh-huh," he murmured, then kissed her on the cheek. "The first step in our courting process, hon. I also made a brief visit to your mother as I wanted to formally ask her permission to court you."

"You did?" Willy said in surprise. "What did she say?"

She turned and walked toward the kitchen.

"She wished me the best of luck and said I really wouldn't need it, if she were reading her youngest daughter correctly." He gave a pleased grin and followed her down the hall.

As she searched for a vase large enough for the roses, he added, "I'd have liked to have been able to ask your father; I'm sorry he's gone. I liked him very much."

Turning from arranging the flowers, Willy replied, "He liked you too, Marsh. He was a big help to me when you and I—when I was trying to understand what had happened to us in the woods that day." She placed the bouquet in the middle of the kitchen table. "There, I'll be able to see them first thing when I come down in the morning."

"Go on, Willy, I'd like to know what he said and how you felt." Marsh removed his suit jacket and hung it on the back of a chair which he pulled out from the table. He sat down, an interested but concerned expression on his face.

She gathered the cellophane wrapper that had been around the roses and put it in the trash basket under the sink, then leaned back against the counter. As it had so many times over the past ten years, that day in Brown's Woods came back to her with vivid clarity.

Marsh had kissed her, not a brotherly peck on the cheek as he often had done, but flat-out square on the mouth. Willy was amazed at him and even more so at herself, as she kissed him back, and she'd never kissed *any* boy on the lips before.

At first, she was startled and hesitant, but suddenly she found her arms wrapped around his neck. Then, Willy felt a warm hand touch the bare skin of her back where her shirt had ridden up. Her instinctive response was to jerk back. At the same time, with a low exclamation of denial, Marsh pushed her away from him, setting her back onto the log.

He stood abruptly and walked quickly away. She was short of breath, and she didn't know if it was from his touch or the acute embarrassment she suddenly felt.

With shaky fingers, she clumsily smoothed down her shirt. *What would he think of her shameless behavior?* She chanced a glance in Marsh's direction.

He had stopped at the edge of the clearing and leaned his hands against the trunk of a large maple tree, his back to her, his usually straight shoulders slumped. She watched him as he took some deep breaths, not quite sure what was the matter with him. She jumped when he uttered some rather coarse expletives, words she had never heard Marsh say in her hearing.

She was upset. Her feelings were so confused, and to make it worse, she felt close to tears.

Marsh stepped away from the tree. Still not looking at her, he muttered, "Let's get home, Willy."

She wiped her eyes on the tail of her shirt, grabbed the poles and his bait bucket, and followed along behind him, carefully keeping her eyes on the path at her feet.

When they reached the road, still not looking at each other, she shoved his fishing pole and bait bucket at him. He took them from her. If he looked at her then, she didn't know, because she didn't lift her eyes from the ground.

"I'm sorry, Willy. I—well, I'm just sorry," he said in a nearly inaudible voice.

She turned to leave him, fresh tears coursing down her cheeks.

"Gosh, don't cry, Willy! It wasn't your fault. I'm older, so it was my fault."

She shook her head and ran blindly down Eden Road, away from Brown's Woods and Marsh. The last thing she heard was his voice calling after her.

"Wait, Willy. Wait!"

She got home, stashed her pole in the shed, and slipped up to her bedroom without anyone seeing her. . . .

"Come and sit at the table with me, Willy."

She crossed to the table and sat at a right angle to his chair. "I was just having a flashback to Brown's Woods, Marsh." She smiled self-consciously at him.

He reached over to take her hand where it lay before her on the tabletop. "I've thought of it often over the years too, Willy. In many ways, it was a traumatic day for us, but an eye-opener as well, at least for me. That day is why I wanted to buy the Brown farm so badly. In my mind, I've always thought of those woods as ours. That was the day that I realized I was in love with you."

Willy gasped in surprise. "You did?"

"I did, sweetheart, and it scared the hell out of me. Oh, I'd always loved you. We'd grown up close; our families were friends; we'd spent so much time together. I'd been the big brother that you didn't have—

darned if I didn't even teach you to tie your shoelaces."

That brought a responsive giggle from Willy. "I remember, you did." She squeezed his hand.

"We made a lot of good memories, didn't we? I hope they are enough to wipe out any lingering bad ones from that day in the woods."

"Oh, yes, Marsh. I was just too young and naive. I'd never been kissed like that before, never on the mouth by *any* boy. My father helped me understand both my reactions and yours. It took me months before I got up the nerve to talk about it, and I may not have even then, but Dad noticed that something was bothering me. Anyway, he drew me out; he had a way of doing that, and we discussed it."

She got up from the table. "I want a glass of water. Would you like one?"

"Yes, please." He watched her as she moved gracefully around the kitchen and thought that he was a lucky man. *Please, let her love me as much as I love her.*

Placing a glass before him, she sat down again. Taking a swallow of her water, she continued. "You'd have thought I would have gone to Mother with my questions, but I believe I instinctively felt that he would be able to explain you to me. I had mostly figured out my own reactions. They ranged from joy in the way you'd made me feel to embarrassment that I'd let you touch me. I felt guilty that I may have done something to cause it all to happen, and anger toward you for even kissing me at all and, consequently, changing our relationship."

Willy paused to sip more water.

Marsh asked, "What did your dad have to say?"

She gave him a little smile. "Well, to put it succinctly, he explained how hormones, particularly in male teenagers, can rage out of control with only the slightest of provocations. He asked me what had led up to the kiss. I told him about it, but it was when I remembered your tickling me at the fishing hole and your abrupt change of mood that he laughed aloud."

Willy blushed a bit and peeked at Marsh who was a little red in the face himself.

"Dad explained how that little episode most likely affected you, and then, at least partly, led to your sudden urge to kiss me later."

Marsh had buried his head in his hands, his shoulders shaking with laughter.

"Bless your dad! He was absolutely right, you know. I had been valiantly trying to still think of you as a kid sister, when all along I was becoming increasingly aware of you as a very appealing, lovely girl on the brink of womanhood. I truly wasn't aware of the depths of my feelings for you until that day."

"I'd always loved you like a brother too, but when I was about thirteen I got this enormous crush on you. I tried to hide it. I thought that you'd not like it at all, or if you knew you'd tease me even more. But Sarah knew—probably Mom as well." She grinned, and Marsh took her hand and kissed it.

"It's strange, Willy, you were the girl I enjoyed being with the most, but I had convinced myself that you only wanted me to be your big brother. Do you know that I nearly got into a couple of fights over you?"

Her eyes widened in surprise and she said in dismay, "No, surely not, Marsh."

"I did. Just a few months before that day, I was in the locker room after track practice, and Jerry Ellison made a crude remark about you and your attributes, shall we say."

It was Willy's turn to bury her red face in her hands. Marsh gently patted her shoulder and continued.

"Jerry was jealous. He liked you, and you wouldn't date him, so he figured I was the reason. Good old Sam got between us or we probably would've both been kicked off the team. Anyway, something Jerry said stuck with me after our tempers cooled, and I'd thought about it all that summer."

Willy looked at him, curiosity showing on her face. "What was it, Marsh?"

"He said that I wasn't fooling him; that I really just wanted you for myself." He grimaced and rose from the table to pace. "At first, I denied it, of course. But as the summer wore on, as I said before, I became more aware of you as a girl, not just my sweet little pretend sister."

"I remember Jerry asking me out, but my folks said no dates until I was sixteen, just in a group like our YF and school things. I told Jerry that, but he must not have believed me." Willy paused and looked up as Marsh stopped pacing to lean back against the sink. "In a way, he was right though. I adored my big brother Marsh, even to the point of daydreaming about you. I'd dream about how I'd grow up one day, and you'd be knocked off your feet by how gorgeous I'd become." She laughed embarrassedly.

"Well, sweetheart, your daydreams came true. Everytime I saw you when I was home from college, I think I loved you a little more. You were so lovely, not just your looks, but the way you were. I wanted so many times to set things right again, but I'd get cold feet and worry that you'd just tell me to get lost." He resumed pacing, his face showing his agitation.

Willy asked in a low, hesitant voice, "Why did you get so angry with me that day in the woods? I mean, now I understand what you were doing when you braced yourself against that tree, but you cursed at me. I could just feel the anger coming off you in waves. I was so hurt and a little afraid of you for a moment or two." Her eyes showed how even the memory of that hurt could upset her.

"Oh, Willy, sweetheart, I wasn't angry at *you*. Not at all." He stopped pacing and leaned his hands on the table opposite her, looking at her over the bouquet of roses. His voice showed his distress when he spoke. "It was me—I was angry at myself. I had lost control, even though only briefly, and I've berated myself ever since for that. Not for kissing you, but for putting my hands on you like I did. You were my trusting little sister, only fifteen years old, for pete's sake, and I was eighteen, about to leave for college. I nearly blew it there."

He resumed a restless pacing around the kitchen. Willy watched in fascination, taking in all that he was telling her.

"I was cursing myself for my own foolishness and stupidity. Standing there, leaning on that tree, I got myself under control, but emotionally I was a wreck. I couldn't even look at you. I was so ashamed of what I'd done, and I just knew that you'd never forgive me. Later on, when I'd see you, I could tell that you didn't feel the same about me anymore. You were uncomfortable around me. Our old friendly, casual relationship was gone, and I blamed myself for that."

He stopped pacing and hunkered down beside her chair.

"Oh, Marsh," she whispered as she brushed back a strand of his hair that had fallen forward. "It wasn't all your fault. It was months before I talked with my dad, and even after that, though I understood better what had happened, I still would get tense and embarrassed around you. I was growing up, as difficult as that is sometimes, and I couldn't seem to handle you. So, I did the only thing I knew how to do—I avoided you as much as possible or made sure other people were always around." She frowned as she added, "I was a coward, I guess. I regret that now."

He took her hands in his and looked into her soft eyes.

"I regret it too, love, but I was the older one. I should have tried harder to fix things. Instead, I let you avoid me, thinking I was helping you. In reality, I was hurting both of us. We wasted so many years," he said in a sad and quiet voice, his thumbs making circles on the backs of her hands.

She smiled lovingly at him. "But that's over. We're together now, and we won't have any more regrets." Willy sighed and lifted one of his hands to press her cheek against it. "I've been wondering, Marsh. What made you sit beside me in church last Sunday?"

He grinned a little guiltily. "I'd heard you were in town, and I'd actually seen you in the woods that Saturday. Seeing you, I knew I had to try again. I knew I loved you, that you were the only woman I'd ever *really* loved. Even if you tossed me out on my ear, I had to try."

"I'm so happy that you did. I was shaking, I was so very nervous, but after a while I relaxed. It began to feel a bit like the old days when we were such good friends."

Marsh gave her hands a gentle squeeze. "You know, you've had a few hours to think about my earlier question over the phone. Since I'm already on bended knee before you, shall I ask it again to make it official?"

Her eyes dancing in anticipation, Willy nodded.

"Dearest Willy, the love of my life. Will you please marry me and make me the luckiest man in Eden?"

Her eyes shining with tears, she replied, "Yes, Marsh, yes. I love you."

Marsh smiled the happiest of smiles, lifted her two hands, and kissed them both. "Thank you, sweetheart, and I love you."

Looking down at Cleo, who had just come over to rub against his ankle, he said, "Did you hear that, old girl? She loves me. But I'd bet you knew that all along, didn't you?"

Cleo gave a little swish of her tail as she ambled away, as if to say, "Of course, you humans are so slow to catch on!"

"How does a December wedding sound, Willy?" Marsh asked, a hopeful look on his handsome face.

"Sounds perfect," she replied as she slipped her arms around his neck.

His voice husky with emotion, Marsh said, "Now, at long last, I can finally kiss you again, the way I've dreamed about for years."

He pulled her forward into his arms, much the same as he had in Brown's Woods so many years ago, and when his mouth covered hers, Willy's heart soared. It was as if those ten years had never been.